# Her Secret Twins

## Janette Foreman

**LOVE INSPIRED**
INSPIRATIONAL ROMANCE

# LOVE INSPIRED®

## INSPIRATIONAL ROMANCE

ISBN-13: 978-1-335-48804-6

Her Secret Twins

Recycling programs
for this product may
not exist in your area.

This edition published by arrangement with Harlequin Books S.A.

For questions and comments about the quality of this book, please contact us at CustomerService@Harlequin.com.

Love Inspired
22 Adelaide St. West, 40th Floor
Toronto, Ontario M5H 4E3, Canada
www.Harlequin.com

Printed in U.S.A.

# "How long are you planning to stay, exactly?"

"Oh, I'm not leaving." Grant met Kallie's stare. "I just found out I'm a dad to twins. You couldn't drag me out of here with a crowbar."

"Are you serious?"

"Dead serious."

Everything she knew was changing.

"You can't hide from this, Kal." His voice was soft. "We're going to have to talk about hard things like custody at some point."

She whirled toward him. "Don't you dare take my children away from me."

His gaze narrowed. "They're *our* children, and who said anything about taking them away?"

But how long until Grant's wanderlust got the better of him and he took off? His sobering gaze met hers.

"I'm not taking them out of your life. We need to be serious about coparenting and somehow making this family thing work."

*Family?* Kallie's mouth ran dry.

"Okay, Kal? You're going to have to trust me on this."

But she *had* trusted him to stick around—after he'd asked her to marry him.

He'd broken that trust. And with it, her heart.

**Janette Foreman** is a former high school English teacher turned stay-at-home mom with a passion for the written word. Through her romances, she hopes people see themselves as having worth in God's eyes. When she sneaks in time for hobbies, she reads, quilts, makes cloth dolls and draws. She makes her home in the northern Midwest with her amazing husband, polydactyl cat, bird-hunting dog and the most adorable baby twin boys on the planet.

### Books by Janette Foreman

### Love Inspired

*Her Secret Twins*

### Love Inspired Historical

*Last Chance Wife*

Visit the Author Profile page at Harlequin.com.

God is our refuge and strength, a very present
help in trouble. Therefore will not we fear,
though the earth be removed, and though the
mountains be carried into the midst of the sea.
—*Psalm* 46:1–2

To James, for your constant love.

To my own sweet twins…what a blessing you are!

To the Lord, for being my refuge and strength
every time the mountains are carried into
the midst of the sea.

# *Chapter One*

That familiar Ford pickup rumbling up the long drive could only mean one thing.

Grant Young had arrived.

Lifting her hands from the sudsy dishwater, Kallie Shore braced herself against the kitchen counter as the rusty blue truck came closer and closer. Was she ready for this? Nearly two years ago, she had stood in this exact spot, watching through the flowery curtains as this pickup's taillights left her South Dakota farm for what she thought had been the last time.

Now he'd returned. Not because he wanted to—she was certain of that. But because he was summoned by the tragedy that would change both of their lives forever.

Wiping her hands on a towel, she dropped her gaze to the envelope on the counter. At their last meeting, the attorney had given it to her while they had discussed the contents of Dad's will. Inside the envelope was a typed note, composed at the end of Dad's life when he had lost the use of his hands. It was his final wish to her, his only child, and it made her ache for him every time she recalled it. *I love you, Kallie Bug. Carry on a better family legacy for the kids than I left behind for you.*

His opinion of himself was skewed, of course. Frank Shore had left her a wonderful legacy. He had been a gentle and hardworking man, who'd loved his farm and had loved his bird dogs. And most important, he had loved her and her thirteen-month-old twins, Ainsley and Peter.

She would do her very best to leave behind a legacy for her kids that Dad would've been proud of—caring for this spread of land until her dying days, then leaving it to the kids. It's what he would have wanted.

A low growl sounded beside her. "Shh, it's okay, Ruby." Kallie reached down to rub her hand over her Llewellin's silky orange ears. "It's only Grant."

Except he wasn't *only Grant*. He was her ex-fiancé. Dad's best former employee. Father to her children.

And unfortunately for Kallie, Dad had willed him half of Bitter Creek Farm.

"He is not coming for us, Ruby. The sooner we remember that, the better," Kallie whispered. "He's only here to make arrangements for his half of our stuff." Whatever he had meant by *arrangements* over the phone, she didn't know. "Hopefully this meeting is quick and painless."

Ruby regarded Kallie with her coppery-brown eyes as if she didn't believe a word Kallie said.

"Truth be told, girl, I don't believe me, either. Now that he's here, we have way too much history to unravel and sift through."

Including the kids she'd never told him about.

Taking in a deep breath, Kallie stepped through the

screen door off the kitchen, Ruby on her heels. For this first meeting, Kallie had sent the kids to spend the afternoon and early evening with her friend Rachel in the town of Bitter Creek, a twenty-minute drive from the farm. It was best this way, Kallie reasoned. She needed to find the right time to tell Grant about them—and, truthfully, a part of her didn't know if she should. Dad had introduced Grant to her as his employee, and they'd hit it off immediately. Fell into a whirlwind romance like nothing she'd ever experienced.

But after one passionate night where they'd gone too far, Grant had left. He'd confessed he wasn't ready for commitment or for life on the farm.

His leaving had felt like betrayal. Like he'd never loved her like she'd loved him.

Kallie descended the porch steps, a breath of summer wind warm on her skin. Maybe she'd only loved him with the excitement of young love. If she had been realistic at the time, maybe she would've realized it never would have worked. He didn't want kids, and his wanderlust would have driven her crazy if he'd lived here—the place that had captured her, heart and soul.

But honestly, what scared her most was the possibility of rejection. What if she told him about the kids and he only rejected them like he had her? Then would it have been better if they'd never met him at all?

The pickup rolled to a stop in the front yard and the driver's-side door opened. She faltered as her foot met gravel, and she clutched the railing.

A boot and pant leg showed beneath the pickup's door, and then a second boot and leg. Grant stepped into view and Kallie's eyes traced the length of him.

Faded denim knees. Trim waist and a button-up Western shirt. Lean muscular arms beneath sleeves rolled to the elbows. Short dark hair framing angular cheeks and green-brown eyes that appeared fierce and wild even if he smiled.

Not that he was smiling yet. He stared back at her with an unreadable expression that made her toes curl inside her slip-on shoes. Inhaling, Kallie tucked a strand of her long blond hair behind her ear. Now or never.

The breeze teased the hem of her sundress as she took the gravel walkway. A backdrop of South Dakota pastures waved green beyond the yard, long-forgotten dog kennels and outbuildings.

"Hey," she said, feeling a little silly sounding casual when she hadn't seen him in so long. If only her voice didn't sound so small.

Grant had one thumb in his jeans pocket, head tilted to keep the sun from his eyes. "Hey, Kallie."

Oh, that voice. Sounded even better in person than it did over the phone. "How was the drive?"

"Not too bad."

"Well, hopefully this trip won't take much of your time. I'll try to keep things brief. Who would've thought we'd end up owning property together? I guess Dad forgot to update his will after we split." She was rambling now—why couldn't she stop? "I guess I just, I don't know—"

"Kallie?"

Pausing, she met his gaze.

"I'm sorry about your dad."

The past two years' struggles came over her in waves

and she barely managed to keep eye contact. Pressing her lips together, she finally glanced away. "Thanks."

"What happened?"

"Wait—the attorney didn't tell you?"

"No."

"Well, Dad was getting worse every month. I mean, sharp as a whip mentally. But his body was giving out on him—"

"But what was it? Cancer? Parkinson's?"

"ALS."

Grant fell silent, closed his eyes, knit his brows together.

A dreaded weight pushed down on Kallie's shoulders. "I'm sorry. I didn't mean to spring the news on you the moment you got here."

"I was only gone two years." His voice sounded scratchy all of a sudden.

"He was diagnosed two Christmases ago."

She could see his jaw muscles working. He looked around as if for an escape, then turned his attention to Ruby, who intently sniffed his tailgate. "Hey, there," he murmured. "You smell my dogs, do ya?" Two kennels stood in his truck bed. Grant worked his fingers through Ruby's hair, his movements showing both his fondness and familiarity with her breed and his intense effort to come to terms with Dad's diagnosis and death.

Truthfully, she hadn't come to terms with it, either. Though she trusted in God's goodness, she didn't understand why He'd allowed such an ugly disease to consume her own father. Dad had been all she'd had. Mom had traveled so much for work as a medical sales rep when Kallie was a kid, and she saw even less of Mom after her parents' divorce. Mom hadn't even come to the funeral.

Sure, she'd tried calling Kallie a few times lately, but Kallie couldn't bring herself to listen to the excuses anymore.

Dwelling on all of that now, however, wasn't going to solve the dilemma she and Grant faced together. They needed to sit down and figure out what to do about the farm.

"So, um…" Kallie swallowed the lump in her throat and jutted her thumb back toward the house. "You're probably beat from driving all day. Why don't you come inside and I'll make up some coffee? We can sit down and discuss everything."

Grant gave Ruby one final rubdown, then stood. "Thanks, but I should get settled in town. My dogs need to eat, and I still need to stop at the dog park to let them release some energy before going to the hotel."

"You're not staying at your parents'?"

Hesitating, he glanced down the road. "No."

She heard the meaning in his voice, his implication that the house was just a shell now that his mom wasn't there.

At four hundred people, Bitter Creek wasn't exactly a metropolis. People's business was often out in the open. She knew his dad—who'd never been able to hold down a job—had drifted off somewhere shortly after Grant left town, and then his mom had moved to Norfolk, Nebraska, to live with Grant's sister, Jill.

"How is your mom?" she asked.

"I'm sure she's doing well—she's a tough cookie."

His gaze dimmed a bit. "I don't get down there to see her as much as I'd like."

One of his dogs barked, which seemed to wake Grant from his thoughts.

"Shouldn't even have their house still," he said, rounding the pickup bed to check on his animals. "It's old and falling apart. Probably more expensive to keep than to sell. But you know Mom—can't let go of anything. And my sister isn't helping." The twinkle in his eye showed he was obviously not as annoyed as he pretended to be. He and Jill had always teased each other, and both loved their mom. Anything of hers would be hard to sell, even if no one lived here anymore. "I'd better head out."

"Wait." Kallie couldn't postpone until later. Rachel only had the kids until their bedtime. "What about discussing the will?"

"It's been a long day. We can do that tomorrow, can't we?"

"But you're already here. You might as well stay. Feed your dogs and let them run."

"Well—"

"It's a *farm*, Grant. There's plenty of space. And half of it is yours, remember?"

"Kallie, come on." He silenced her with his words, and suddenly she understood.

He'd intended to stay and talk things out, but being here overwhelmed him. She saw it in his eyes, the way he kept glancing at the road. Was he remembering how they'd left things? Or was thinking about Dad so painful that he needed to do it alone? Dad had been more like a father to Grant than his own had ever been.

Kallie glanced at her watch. Half-past four o'clock. She raised her gaze to meet his, hoping she could instill him with courage. "Please, Grant? Can you come inside for just a minute? It shouldn't take long to figure things out. Then tomorrow, you can be on your way back to Iowa, if you'd like."

Hands in pockets, he worked his jaw muscles again. The telltale sign he was thinking things through and was uncomfortable with the situation. Kallie wanted to scoff at the irony. Whatever tension he felt right now, she was pretty sure she could top it.

Finally, he conceded. "I guess it would be good to get it done tonight. I have some business in Bitter Creek tomorrow, and then I need to get on the road."

He freed his dogs from their kennels, allowing them to roam while he followed her to the house. The screen door closed against its frame with a *knock* as they entered the kitchen, where the aroma of slow cooker chicken thickened the air.

Grant's gaze wandered. "The place hasn't changed much, I see."

"No, it hasn't." At least, not the house itself. And she'd stashed away all the baby memorabilia for the time being—until after she knew what Grant was all about.

"I keep thinking Frank's going to come around the corner, though."

At Grant's words, Kallie felt her throat begin to close. If this had been years earlier, she would have sought refuge in his arms. But things were different now. Turning to a cabinet, she took down a coffee mug. "Still like it black?"

"Yep."

She reached for the fresh carafe of coffee.

"Do you still train Llewellins during the summer?" he asked.

"No, we quit when Dad's health worsened. All we have left now is Ruby."

"Oh." She heard him take a seat at the table.

Honestly, it was fine by her that there weren't a bunch of dogs on site all summer anymore. It added a lot of extra work—Dad enjoyed it, and for that reason, Kallie had been happy to help. But for her, Ruby was the only Llewellin setter she needed. A loveable couch potato who occasionally wanted to run and explore the fields. Nothing complicated or high-maintenance. And right now with the kids so little, Kallie couldn't afford any more painstaking tasks.

"I saw you in *Bird Dog* magazine."

He chuckled, sounding a little embarrassed. "Yeah, well, you'd better frame that because it'll become a limited edition. You're not going to see another one."

"I'm sure with your growing popularity you'll get into it again." Crossing her arms, she leaned a hip against the counter. "Honestly, I'm surprised you came out here, rather than finalizing things over the phone. Your life is busy. And being the first of June, surely you have a whole schedule of training clinics to get to, right?"

Her moxie surprised her. As a general rule, she avoided confrontation at all costs. But having Grant here put her on edge, which apparently caused her to lose control of her words.

He traced his finger along the rim of his mug, taking a second to answer. "I'm on my way to a clinic this weekend, actually. In Wyoming. Figured the farm was on the way."

"Sure."

She should have known that's why he'd stopped by. It was on the way to something else.

Time to get ahold of herself and remember he'd only come to discuss the will. Grant had a successful life outside this place. According to the magazine interview, he'd been living in Iowa all this time as the executive director of a nonprofit rescue dog facility dedicated to helping setters in desperate need. And when he wasn't at the facility, he was on the road putting on bird dog training clinics. Traveling a lot, and loving every minute of it, the article clearly pointed out. He obviously worked hard living his dream, and becoming so successful in a matter of two years was likely the reason behind his publicity.

And it wasn't a career sustainable for a family man. *Grant wasn't a family man.*

"At any rate," he continued, "I'll be out of your hair as quickly as possible. I just wanted to come out here and tell you I'm sorry about Frank and that I'm not going to accept the inheritance."

Kallie's brows shot up, her thoughts derailing. "Are you serious? You don't want your half?"

Grant shrugged and for a second, it looked as if his thoughts warred behind his gaze. "I don't know what I would do with it. I can't keep it. I mean, you and me owning the same spread of land…" He trailed off, then seemed to gather his thoughts and head in a different direction. "It's just not a good idea. You can understand that, right?"

She straightened away from the counter. "I guess I can."

"Great. Glad that's settled, then."

"Yeah, great."

Settled. Is that what they were?

It sounded so cold, so final. But then, wasn't that how their relationship was now? And thankfully, he hadn't claimed his inheritance only to turn around and sell his half. She'd been afraid that would happen—because if anyone bought the land, it would *have to be her.* Otherwise, she wouldn't be able to afford to stay here, either. Not that she could afford this land if it went up for sale. Money was already tight, due to Dad's medical bills and the loan he took out to pay for seeds this year. She still needed to sit down and calculate everything—his assets compared to his outstanding balance.

Coffee mugs in hand, they lingered in silence. Kallie watched Grant as her heart squeezed. All their memories, a few triumphs and many regrets, floated between them. Present yet unacknowledged. Was she supposed to ignore them like they'd never mattered? She'd almost married this man.

One thing was certain. No matter how quick this meeting went with Grant Young, it certainly wasn't going to be painless.

A knock sounded on the door.

"Hello?" Rachel's voice carried through the screen.

Kallie's heart dropped. She rushed to the door. Rachel stood there with a baby car seat carrier placed on either side of her on the porch.

"Rachel," she hissed, hoping Grant couldn't hear

her—though hiding was futile at this point. "You weren't supposed to be here until seven."

"Seven?" Rachel's eyes widened. "You're kidding! I thought you said by five."

*Five?* Dear Rachel Whethers had always been a little scatterbrained, but this was over the top even for her. "No, I need longer than that." She heard Grant's chair shift. "Please, Rach. Take them somewhere. Anywhere."

Concern crossed Rachel's face, a slight breeze picking up strands of her dark hair. "What's going on? You okay?"

"That Rachel Gunsing I hear?" Grant appeared over Kallie's shoulder.

Rachel made eye contact through the screen, and suddenly understanding bloomed across her face. "Grant Young. Well, that's a surprise I'd never expected." She glanced at Kallie as if in question, and Kallie shook her head in response. Rachel turned back to Grant. "I'm actually Rachel Whethers now. Got married to Kyle eighteen months ago."

"That's great, Rach." He reached around Kallie for the door. "Why don't you stop in and catch up?"

Kallie's heart rate tripped. "Oh, I'm sure that's not necessary. She's probably pretty busy—"

Grant eyed her. "She drove the twenty minutes from town to stand on your doorstep for thirty seconds? I don't think so."

"Actually, I do need to be going." Apology slashed her friend's gaze. "Kyle's taking me out for my birthday tonight since I have to work on the actual day."

Just then, Peter began to cry, no doubt eager to get out of his seat.

Kallie cringed. Grant glanced at the babies for the first time, and his brows rose. She closed her eyes and offered up a silent prayer for mercy.

Grant Young glanced between the two car seat carriers on the porch, then back up at Rachel Whethers. No doubt about it, things sure had changed in the span of two years. Last time he saw Rachel, they were all newly out of high school, and she'd been full of life and totally disinterested in settling down.

And now it seemed she'd become a mom.

"Twins?" he asked.

Rachel began to pale before glancing at Kallie. "Yep."

And Kallie. Grant couldn't believe how seeing her again had nearly knocked him flat as he'd stepped out of his pickup.

He wasn't exactly sure why he'd traveled all the way out to the farm just to tell her his simple plans regarding his half of the inheritance. He supposed a piece of him really wanted a reason to see the place again, to remember Frank in the environment the man had loved so deeply and to offer his condolences to Kallie. And, of course, he was curious how she had fared these past two years and what she was up to these days.

But now, after sitting in her kitchen and drinking from a random mug he actually remembered, he realized it was a huge mistake. Emotions he'd assumed were long buried had begun to resurface the instant he saw her standing on the walkway, her sweet blue eyes and waist-length blond hair tucked behind her ear. Man, she still looked good. Sounded good. Still fit snugly into a pocket he hadn't realized lay open in his heart.

A pocket he knew he needed to close forever. Because he and Kallie would never work. He'd left here a young man scared of commitment and full of big ambitions— and he'd always regretted it.

Growing up with a bum for a father had scared him into believing he'd repeat the man's mistakes. That he wouldn't be a good husband to Kallie and wouldn't be a good father if they ever had kids.

So at the time, it was easier to run away. But he'd been wrong to do it. She deserved better treatment than that. Now here he was, a bit washed up and lost, looking to regain his sense of direction. But he needed to remember he wasn't going to find that here.

Rachel coughed softly into her fist, standing there awkwardly, like she wasn't sure what to do next, which only served to make Grant suspicious. What was going on and why wouldn't she come in?

He was about to ask when the phone in his pocket chimed. Cell service was nonexistent out here, so it had to be Kallie's Wi-Fi. Hmm, an email. How about that? His phone remembered this place and had automatically connected.

Quietly he excused himself to check the email. As he did, Kallie scurried out onto the porch, her voice hushed as she asked something of Rachel.

Who knew what they were discussing. Turning his attention to the phone, Grant opened his inbox. The email was from Will Parker, his contact for the Helping Hands board of directors, responding to Grant's question of whether or not they'd held their meeting yet—

the one they were supposed to have last week in order to okay the plans for the facility's office rebuild, which they'd lost in a fire earlier this year. Something had postponed last week's meeting, though he didn't know what, and they'd promised to hold a new one today.

Grant,
No meeting yet. Waiting on some measures to finalize before we meet. Perhaps next week.
—Will

Grant frowned. Not the answer he'd anticipated, for sure. He tapped out a reply.

Finalize measures? What kind of measures?

Kallie opened the screen door, so Grant slipped his phone into his jeans pocket. He froze in his movement, though, when he noticed her hefting one of the carrier seats. Rachel came in behind her with the other one.

Okay, so maybe she was staying for a visit after all.

Grant stepped out of the way, watching the two women head to the living room and unload two dark-haired babies onto the carpet. A boy crawled toward a stuffed giraffe Kallie handed him, and a girl toddled quickly after him before also dropping to her knees.

"Well," Rachel glanced hesitantly at Grant before sending Kallie a look, "I'll see you Sunday."

"Thanks for watching the kids, Rach."

Grant blinked. *Wait, what?*

Rachel brushed thick hair over her shoulder, and

inched back toward the screen door, peeking at Grant as she retreated past him. "Safe trip back to Iowa."

"Um, thanks." He watched her go before turning back to the living room.

Was Kallie a mom?

And was she married? Grant glanced around the kitchen for any sign of a male's presence. A work coat or muddy boots or even a family photo taped to the fridge. But nothing.

His focus returned to the babies making themselves at home, and he was suddenly aware of the muscles tightening in his stance. Stiffly, he made his way into the living room, lingering just inside the doorway, eyesight never leaving the twins.

This made no sense. Was there a guy? There must not be because otherwise, why would Frank will half of the farm to Grant? Actually, regardless of whether or not Kallie was seeing someone or married or whatever, he had no idea why Frank had left Grant in the will. But especially if some guy's kids were involved. Unless Grant was…

*No.* No. That couldn't be the case. These kids were little, and he'd been gone two years. He had no real experience with babies, but he'd guess they were only seven or eight months old.

After a couple of long, deep breaths, he found his voice. "So—they're yours?"

Kallie looked into his eyes. She nodded, and even though that was the answer he'd expected, something in Grant's world still knocked sideways.

*Who…?*

No, he couldn't ask that question out loud. It was·

brash. Besides, he wasn't sure he wanted to know the answer. Didn't keep his mind from scrolling through the possibilities. There weren't many—Kallie hadn't dated anyone before Grant. Someone new must have come to town.

Oh. Except for Brendan Millard.

Grant clenched his jaw and lowered himself onto the sofa, the same one he'd used when he'd worked here, and Frank would encourage him to take a quick nap after lunch before returning to the tractor.

Brendan Millard's parents ran the neighboring farm, and he'd grown up with Kallie. From the beginning, he hadn't been a fan of Grant, who'd moved to Bitter Creek in high school and was a grade older than both of them. Grant suspected, though, it was because Brendan's feelings for her ran deeper than friendship.

Grant rubbed at his temple and then down his shadowed jaw. The kids had to be Brendan's. She would have told Grant if they were his.

Right?

"This is Peter," Kallie said, her voice soft, bringing Grant's thoughts around. "And this is Ainsley. Peter's older by nine minutes, but Ainsley acts like she's in charge."

Peter threw a burp cloth over his head, and giggling a silvery laugh, Ainsley joyously yanked it off, causing them both to squeal.

Grant couldn't help but smile a little. "They're cute."

"Thanks."

Watching, Grant felt pummeled. Kallie had always insisted Brendan was just a friend, but what if that hadn't been the case? Had he stepped in after Grant left? It would make sense. Brendan loved to farm. And he had a bunch of siblings. He was built for family.

Two things that weren't in Grant's blood—no matter how hard he'd searched for them years ago, when his relationship with Kallie had depended on it.

But where was Brendan now?

"We should feed the dogs," Kallie said suddenly, rising to her feet, Ainsley in her arms. "I'll grab the stroller from the truck bed if you don't mind bringing Peter."

"Oh. Sure." He scooped up the little boy, so light he worried about squashing him. *Relax, Young. He's not a newborn pup.*

He followed Kallie outside, heading for her truck parked in the turnaround. "I'm surprised Peter's doing as well as he is, since he doesn't know you," she said over her shoulder.

"Why? Is he generally shy?" And why had she asked him to carry the child if she knew that about him? Grant looked at Peter in his arms, but the boy only squinted in the sun, distracted by the outdoors.

"Generally." Kallie placed Ainsley on the grass so she could open the tailgate and pull out a folded double-wide stroller. "He loves people, but he has to warm up first."

Ainsley quickly approached the stroller, seemingly recognizing it. Kallie unfolded it and lifted her daughter into one of the seats, then buckled her in. Grant brought Peter over and followed suit, albeit awkwardly.

"Do they like this thing?"

"They love it. I do, too."

"Is it hard to maneuver around here?"

"Actually, it's easy." She checked the stroller's visors so the sun wasn't in the kids' eyes, then pushed the stroller across the turnaround. "It's a sport utility stroller, so the tires are really nice. We use it all the time."

The kids kicked their legs and pointed out scenery as they rumbled over the gravel and dirt.

As they approached the barn, a Llewellin skittered out of the shadows and loped toward them.

"Hey, Chief." Grant kept up with Kallie and the stroller, though a couple of yards to her right. "You remember Chief, right?" He motioned to the bird dog as Chief's nose tugged him toward a stand of scrub oaks.

"I do. Took me a moment. He's from the same litter as Ruby, I think."

"Yep." Grant slid his hands deep into his pockets, gravel scraping beneath his boots. When he'd worked here just out of high school, Frank held summer camps for training bird dogs, and in the winter, he guided hunters. The South Dakota prairie teemed with pheasants and grouse. One winter, some hunters had sold Frank a pair of Llewellins, and Grant had purchased Chief from their first litter.

He led the way into the barn where the dog food was kept, and Kallie followed, Chief slipping in between them.

"Do you remember where we keep the food?"

Instead of answering, he simply took keys from a nail on the wall and unlocked a cabinet beneath the worktable. Then he pulled out the tub of food.

Chief ran the length of the barn, joining Bella, his second setter who was too busy checking out all the new smells to acknowledge their presence.

"Did you get your other dog from your shelter?"

"Yep. That's Bella. She's gun-shy, but we do well together."

He called her over and Bella approached with obvious fondness. Depositing the keys on the worktable, he knelt and buried his fingers in the tri-colored hair behind her ears. Bella closed her eyes and tilted her head toward him. Then he scooped food into a dish, and at the sound of food hitting metal, Chief was hot on Bella's trail, looking for his own supper. Grant fed him, too.

"A previous handler spooked her while hunting. An all-too-common problem with our shelter dogs, I'm afraid."

"Do you like working at the rescue facility?"

"I do. It's fulfilling to witness so many success stories, you know?" He dropped some food in a bowl for Ruby. "We have it set up where setters are taken into foster homes for a while before they can be adopted. This helps us evaluate their true nature in a home environment. Plus, it gives them the comfort of a home while they wait for a permanent family."

"Is that how you found Bella? Did you foster her?"

"Yep. And once I looked into her big eyes, I was a goner."

Much like Kallie. He'd known she was special the moment he saw her.

Clearing his throat, Grant turned away and locked the dog food back in the cupboard, where it was safe from raccoons who sometimes explored the barn at night.

Call him soft but he had a love for the setters who needed extra understanding and attention. He'd found that passion while working here at Bitter Creek Farm, and when he'd gotten involved in Iowa training them and running the rescue facility, he'd realized he enjoyed caring for someone other than himself.

It had awakened an instinct he'd never thought possible.

The truth ricocheted down through his core as he straightened, letting the dogs eat. Because he feared becoming like his dad, he'd never wanted kids. And when he and Kallie had gotten carried away one night, the reality of marriage and the possibility of fatherhood had hit him hard.

That night had woken him up, made him believe that he couldn't be what Kallie deserved.

But now…

He glanced at Kallie and her kids, at the life he could have had if only he'd had the courage. All of this could have been his—this simple life, with their own family to come home to rather than an empty apartment. But he'd missed that opportunity, and someone else had taken his place.

He only had himself to blame.

# Chapter Two

"Thanks for letting me stick around for supper, Kallie."

"No problem."

Though honestly, Kallie didn't feel as nonchalant as her answer indicated. Ever since Grant had arrived, she'd been flooded with guilt. Back when he left, she'd felt justified in keeping the kids a secret. He'd wanted to forget farm life and train dogs. Wasn't interested in being a dad or a husband. Not to mention the teensy-tiny detail that he'd flat out left her barely a month after proposing.

She still worried that he wouldn't care. That he'd shrug the kids off. So, she'd held her tongue through supper preparation and getting the kids into their high chairs. To keep her mind busy, she worked with her hands—grabbed various pots and bowls of food from the counter to bring them to the table.

Grant watched her from his chair. "Can I help you with anything?"

"No, I'm almost done." The tasks didn't need to be completed any faster than they already were.

Peter and Ainsley sat in matching high chairs beside her place setting. Cooked mashed peas littered their trays, and thankfully, they ate in pure delight—judging by their screeching and their attempts to share the peas across their trays.

More landed on the floor between them than anywhere else, which Ruby appreciated.

The oven timer beeped, so Kallie bent and pulled out the chicken potpie, the center boiling through a cracked edge of crust. She'd used the chicken from her slow cooker, thinking with Grant staying that the meal needed to be heartier than she'd originally planned. She set it in the middle of everything else like a centerpiece at a Thanksgiving feast.

She finally sat, and Grant said a prayer. And after saying "Amen," she silently added another prayer for strength and wisdom. In high school and while she dated Grant, she hadn't been very faithful in her spiritual life. But since the kids were born, and especially in recent months, she'd learned a lot about God's everlasting goodness. And drawing from the deep well of His love comforted her like nothing else ever had. If anyone could help her know how to handle this situation, it would be Him.

"All this food for just us?" Grant eyed the smorgasbord. "You know my stomach's shrank since I stopped working on the farm."

A tiny smile tugged on her lips before she stuffed it away. She'd spent some of her nervous energy on cooking, and yep, one look around the table and she knew she'd gone a tad overboard.

She dished more peas onto her plate to squish with her fork for the kids. "Dig in."

Apparently she didn't need to tell him twice. He took a long swig of his ice water and helped himself to a steaming biscuit to slather with butter and honey.

"So, I've been thinking. Have you thought about hiring a farm hand for the summer?" He spooned potpie onto his plate. "Come July, it'll be way too hot to cart the kids everywhere for hours on end."

Free advice often fell flat, and this was no exception. Kallie didn't look up from distributing more peas to the kids. "We have air conditioning in the work truck."

"That old thing? You can't rely on it working when the temps hit over one hundred."

"We did last year when Dad was sick."

"Well, last year you didn't have a choice. But no kids should ride around the farm in that old beater, not in the middle of summer."

She stared at him. "The truck is fine, Grant."

"You say that now. Wait until it's noon, and you break down in the middle of a pasture. It could become a bad situation very fast."

"Enough, okay?"

She gritted her teeth to not say any more. He couldn't just leave her one day and then waltz back into her life two years later giving orders. She left the table for more milk from the fridge. While she refilled Ainsley's and Peter's sippy cups, heavy silence weighed her down. This was going to be even harder than she'd thought.

"Sorry, Kal."

Kallie turned from the counter, sippy cups in hand. "What?"

He ran his hand over his brow, then down his face. "I've got a lot on my plate right now, so I'm just on edge. The last few months have been brutal. A fire destroyed Helping Hands Kennel, the rescue I run."

Kallie's eyes widened, her skepticism falling away as she sank into her chair. "Oh, that's horrible. Where are all the dogs?"

"Some are still with their foster families. But some families pulled out. Those dogs are at a friend's animal sanctuary outside Waterloo, the next city over. I'll get them back once I have a facility again." He exhaled. "We have nineteen Llewellins and English setters waiting for permanent homes right now. Nineteen. And the adoption process is slower when we're working out of a makeshift facility."

"That's a lot of dogs. How will the facility make a difference if your policy is for dogs to stay with foster families?"

"Well, I can't take on new dogs until we have places to foster them. But I've called around, and I keep getting the same answer from potential foster families— they don't see us as a legitimate business. I mean, I can't blame them. You should see the run-down office we're using right now. We need a bit more professionalism before people will take us seriously." He sighed. "I'm hitting some snags getting the new facility up and running."

Peter tossed his spoon. Kallie bent to retrieve it. "What kind of snags? Can't you simply rebuild?"

"I guess not. My board of directors wants to meet before they'll allow the funding to be used for the facility. My contact at the board said they've got some stipulations they're looking into." He shook his head. "I have no idea what that means, and so far, my contact hasn't returned my latest email. I'll have to call tomorrow on my way to Wyoming."

He returned to his meal. Kallie put the spoon back on Peter's tray.

Ainsley squawked and pounded her tray, out of food. Kallie dumped some more peas in front of her, feeling Grant's eyes on her. Peter called out for more peas, too.

"Can't I help you with anything?"

Ainsley dropped her sippy cup, and Kallie bent over.

The cup touched Grant's foot. He stooped over and grabbed it. Kallie sat up in her chair again, stretching out her hand over the table to get it back.

Grant eyed both kids, and the nerves piled up inside her as she set Ainsley's drink on her tray. This charade was pointless—he was bound to figure things out and she'd been stupid to hide it from him.

"How's Brendan Millard these days?"

Blinking, Kallie frowned. "What? Fine, I guess."

Peter tossed his empty cup and cried for more.

"What's he up to?"

Kallie disappeared beneath the table. "Running his farm, like everyone else around here." She snatched Peter's cup and stood to refill it.

"He's not hanging around here?"

"Why would he?"

"I just figured he'd be available for you and the kids."

Ainsley cried out, out of peas again.

"Here." Grant pushed his chair back. "Let me help."

"No, you're a guest. Sit down." Kallie shoveled peas onto the tray. But Ainsley waved her arms, batting away Kallie's spoon, sending her cup over the edge again.

She gasped as the lid came off, spilling milk across the floor.

Grant popped up from his seat.

"I've got it." Kallie darted for the paper towel roll on the counter, but he snatched it first. He swooped in on the milk spreading over the linoleum.

She knelt beside him. "Let me do it."

"I can handle a spill…"

"But—"

"Go eat. You've hardly touched your food."

"No. I'm going to do it." She snatched the paper roll from him. "Now tell me why Brendan Millard would be here for me and the kids?"

"Aren't these his kids?"

"No, Grant."

Freezing, he raised his gaze to meet hers. "Then whose are they?"

Her eyes widened. Did he honestly have no idea? She took a couple of deep breaths, then stood. She set Ainsley's sippy cup on the table with a distinct *tap* and turned to the counter, tugging saran wrap off a pan of dessert. "Brownie?"

"Kal."

He wasn't playing around. Turning, she met his dark eyes and willed herself not to flinch. Time for the truth. "They're yours."

"Grant, stop."

The screen door shut behind him as Grant stalked down the steps. He needed air.

Returning to Bitter Creek Farm had already been hard, dredging up memories of training setters with Frank and learning about life. Falling in love with Kallie—hard and fast. But this? Finding out he'd been a father all this time? That was harder still.

"Grant." Kallie followed him outside. "Let me explain."

"What's there to explain? I understand what's going on here. You lied to me about everything. That about covers it, right?"

"Please."

He paused to face her, spying her on the porch—slip-on shoes, breeze tossing her long blond hair. Her slender wrists and fingers. The freckles dotting her bare shoulders. He distinctly remembered touching those shoulders as they danced in the moonlight together...

That night when their perfect world had completely ruptured.

"I wanted to tell you so many times. But—"

"But what? The timing never felt right?"

"No."

"Why'd you keep them a secret, Kallie?"

Her gaze turned steely, arms crossing over her middle. "Why'd you leave me a month after asking me to marry you?"

"Don't change the subject."

"I'm not. It's one of the reasons I didn't tell you." Her eyes misted over. "You left me. And you did *not* want kids. I didn't know what to do."

Twins. The news still shook through him. He'd seen the kids, the color of their hair, but he'd reasoned away any chance they could've been his. Kallie's gaze pleaded with him to understand, but it was a whole lot of information to take in at once.

"I did do that. And I'm very sorry. But you should have told me. I still have my same phone, or you could have called Jill—"

"I don't know. I guess I figured you were better off not knowing."

"That's the problem, Kallie. You decided this important thing for me. You can't do that. You can't control everything. I had a right to know."

A tear slipped down her cheek, and he fell silent. Was she just now feeling bad about all of this or had she tormented herself for years? He closed his eyes against the regret shuddering through his chest. Regret over their past mistakes and the mistake he was making now. No matter what she'd done to him, he didn't need to belittle her.

The way she stood there, hand nervously gripping her opposite bicep, she looked exactly the same as when he left years ago. Alone and scared. Needing him as he walked away.

He was guilty of hurting her, too.

Grant rubbed the back of his neck. One little statement: *They're yours.* Suddenly, his life would never be the same. His mind swirled with hurt, with anger, with questions. But one thing he knew for sure. Those kids needed a dad. Grant had one physically, but not actively. He was scared to death of repeating the man's mistakes.

In fact, he'd already started. He'd been absent for their entire lives. But not anymore.

He headed for his pickup.

She followed him. "Where are you going?"

"To find some cell service to call my hotel."

"Why?"

"To cancel my reservation."

He heard her feet skid to a halt on the gravel. "You're leaving already? You're mad that I didn't tell you about the kids and yet you're already leaving?"

"Hardly." He hopped into his truck and shut the door, staring down at her through the half-rolled window. "Just the opposite. I'm coming out to the farm."

Her brows shot up. "I don't think so. You're not staying here."

"You're right, I'm not. I'll be in the employee cottage."

She stared at him.

"What? It's still standing, right?"

"Yeah, it's still standing. But it needs work. I don't think you want to stay there."

"There you go making decisions for me again," he said. "I'm not worried about the work. Just want to be close to my kids." He stuck his key in the ignition and turned it, revving his engine to life. "See ya in a few."

Kallie didn't look happy, but she'd just have to be okay with it. Starting today, she was going to see a whole lot more of Grant Young. He wouldn't let his kids grow up like he had—without a relationship with their dad.

The white broken line down Interstate 90 stretched to the horizon. Grant hadn't expected to see this section of South Dakota prairie again so soon. But when you had to drive to the next exit in order to find a cell signal, that's what you did.

Once he sat on the side of the road, just after the off ramp, he called the hotel and canceled his reservation. Then he called the hosts of every clinic he'd planned to give this summer to cancel until further notice. Until he could figure out what was going on in his life.

Even with his phone calls completed, though, he wasn't ready to go back to the farm. Not just yet. He still needed to process this new load of information for a few more minutes. He wound up calling his sister, Jill.

"Well, that's just about the craziest news I think I've ever heard," Jill said.

"Yeah." Grant ran his finger along the edge of his pickup's radio, wiping away dust that had collected there since he'd last detailed this old thing. "I'm still stunned."

"Me, too. And I'm just your sister. I can't imagine how you feel." She paused. "So, I'm not trying to be rude here—but are you sure they're yours?"

Grant shrugged, even though he knew no one could see him except the rolling prairie out his open window. "They have brown eyes and brown wavy hair. The more I think about it, the more I'm realizing Peter looks a lot like me in that picture of us. You know, the one that used to hang in Mom and Dad's hall."

"Are you going to get a paternity test?"

His brows scrunched. "Do I need to?"

"I would."

"Why would Kallie tell me they're mine if they aren't? She doesn't accept help from me, and she clearly doesn't want me here. The only reason I even found out is because Frank left me in his will."

Which certainly made him wonder. He'd been added as a beneficiary when he and Kallie got engaged, but he figured with their breakup he'd been taken off—like normal ex-fiancés. Had it slipped Frank's mind or had he left Grant in the will on purpose, so he'd learn about the kids one way or another?

Reality hit him hard and heavy. "What rights do I even have to them anyway? We're not married. I know they're mine, but I've been absent all of their life. They know and trust Kallie, and that's it."

"Not knowing about them isn't entirely your fault, though. She should have told you," Jill said. "Listen, I was talking with a friend of mine here in Norfolk, who's going through something kind of like this, and he said fathers have rights, too. You'll have to check South Dakota laws, but I think all you have to do is establish you're their biological father. Then you'll have all the rights and responsibilities of a parent."

His sister, hairstylist-turned-lawyer all of a sudden. "Like child support and visitation?"

"Yeah, and like, custody."

Custody. Wow, this was getting real. And fast.

He exhaled. Turned his gaze to the setting sun. "This is a lot to process, Jill."

"I'm sure it is." Jill paused. "Just promise me one thing."

"What?"

"Don't let Kallie push you out of their lives again, okay? You've already lost precious time you can't get back. Make the most of the time you have now."

Grant exhaled. "That's my plan."

"Okay. Hey, Grant?" Jill's voice softened. "Congratulations. I'm excited to meet them. I'm sure Mom will be, too."

A smile slid up Grant's face. "Thanks. That means a lot."

When he hung up, he started his pickup. Jill was right. Kallie had already denied him access to important milestones. He wouldn't let that happen again.

He didn't know all the details yet, but as surely as he drove back to Bitter Creek Farm, he was bound and determined to never let Peter and Ainsley go.

After finishing supper and bathing the children, Kallie strapped Peter and Ainsley into the stroller and trekked down to the cottage.

As she'd expected, she found Grant's truck parked out front, and Chief sitting on the front porch, soaking up the sun and taking in the change of scenery. He ran to greet them as they neared, and Kallie gave him a few quick rubs behind the ear.

Peter squealed and pointed at Chief, and Kallie managed a smile. Her kids held a wonder for the world that she'd lost in recent years. What would it be like to feel that way about life again?

The door to the cottage swung open, Grant leaning on the doorframe. Bella scurried over after him, greeting the kids and Kallie. "Well, hey there, neighbor," Grant said with a wink. "Welcome to my humble abode."

The smile slid off Kallie's face. Just how long was he planning on staying?

But her lack of enthusiasm didn't seem to faze him. "Come in." He approached the stroller. "Hey, bud." He unstrapped Peter and lifted him into his arms.

But Peter squirmed and reached out for Kallie, trying to wriggle from Grant's grip.

"Like I said, he's pretty shy around strangers."

Grant bounced Peter a little, probably in an attempt to cheer him up. "We won't be strangers for long." He turned and headed into the house, calling for Chief and Bella to follow him. Kallie stifled a sigh as she unstrapped Ainsley and followed. Stopping by the cottage was probably the wrong thing to do, but if she hid from whatever issue was building between her and Grant, then it would grow and grow. Much better to nip it in the bud right now, rather than let it get out of control.

*You can't control everything...*

She didn't want to think about Grant's words, so instead, she stepped inside and focused on the cottage's aged surroundings.

"I think this place will work well." Grant glanced back at her before surveying the room. "Though I might need to borrow some sheets until my online order gets here."

Online order? What did Grant Young think he was doing—moving in?

Looking around, she suddenly felt weary. The last time anyone stayed here was about a year ago—an employee working for Dad about a year after Grant left. The man had only stuck around for a few months before going someplace warmer. Texas or Oklahoma, she couldn't remember. Though a few months had apparently been long enough to put a hole through the wall, destroy some window blinds beyond repair, chip the counter and knock the screen door off its hinges.

Rachel had watched the kids so Kallie could at least surface clean this place after the employee left, but that's as far as she'd gotten. And unfortunately, by then, she'd been the only one who could've worked on the cottage because Dad wasn't able-bodied. She could have hired someone to help, but that had just been too much to deal with at the time.

No way could she handle a list of repairs right now just because Grant had decided he didn't want to stay in town.

Then again, she reminded herself she didn't *need* to repair things right now, because Grant wasn't going to be here that long. Obviously longer than she'd thought, but not for forever.

Grant shifted Peter higher in his arms, but the poor boy wasn't interested in staying with him. Grant set him on the floor and let him toddle into the living room. Kallie wrinkled her nose. "I haven't had a chance to clean that carpet."

"He should be fine, right?"

She eyed Grant, not amused. He seemed to get the message and picked Peter up again. They moved out to the porch and let the kids down to look around. A faint breeze whispered in the cottonwoods nearby, intermingling with the distant song of sparrows and finches. Kallie longed to relax into it, but how could she when Grant rattled her?

"So…" Breaking the silence, his voice came quietly as they stared over the expanse of prairie and trees. "When's their birthday?"

"May third," she said.

"What are their full names?"

"Peter Allen and Ainsley Elise."

"When did they take their first steps?"

Her heart began to tug. "Eleven months."

"First words?" His voice sounded gravelly this time, and a burn started behind Kallie's eyes.

"Ainsley says 'Mama,' but Peter hasn't said anything discernible yet."

"Well, soon, they'll learn 'Daddy,' too."

Kallie closed her eyes. "It takes a while for them to learn new words at this stage, Grant."

"I don't mind."

"How long are you planning to stay, exactly?"

"Oh, I'm not leaving." He matched her stare. "I just found out I'm a dad to twins. You couldn't drag me out of here with a crowbar and a winch." He turned to face her full on. "And another thing. I've decided to keep my half of the inheritance. I'm planning to pay child support, and I'm getting a paternity test and seeking joint custody."

"Are you serious?"

"Dead serious."

Fear rippled through her, the surety of his list shaking her foundation. Everything she knew was changing so fast. Too fast. Turning on her heel, she scooped up the children, then marched down the porch steps and deposited them inside the stroller.

Her hands shook as she tried to secure their harnesses. Grant's boot falls sounded behind her.

"You can't hide from this, Kal." This time, his voice was soft yet firm. "We're going to have to talk about things like custody at some point."

She whirled toward him. "Don't you dare take my children away from me!"

His gaze narrowed. "They're *our* children, and who

said anything about taking them away? I'm staying right here on the farm, remember?"

Yes, she remembered. But how long until his wanderlust got the better of him and he decided to take off? He was only here for the kids, not for her. There was nothing keeping him on the farm. "What about your job in Iowa? I thought you loved it."

"I do." He shrugged. "I'll try working it from here for a while, see what happens. I'll figure something out." His sobering gaze met hers. "I'm not taking them out of your life. It's not right for them to grow up without a dad, but it's also not right to be without a mom. We need to be serious about coparenting and somehow making this family thing work."

Family? Kallie's mouth ran dry. How could they possibly become something like that?

"Okay, Kal? You're going to have to trust me on this."

What could she say? Nothing made sense in her jostled thoughts. She said good-night and pushed the kids back toward her house. Because the truth was, she *had* trusted him to stick around—after he'd asked her to marry him. He'd broken that trust. And with it, her heart.

The stroller's wheels crunched softly over the gravel in an otherwise soundless evening, the moon high overhead. Any summer night that she came outside and saw the moon positioned here, she thought about Grant. Counting stars in his truck bed and eating s'mores around homemade campfires. Talking about life, love and the future. So many good memories under that moon. So many slipups, too. Two flawed human beings trying to forge ahead into a marriage when they'd had no idea how to do so effectively.

And now he was planning to stay on the farm. For the foreseeable future. For the kids.

She should be happy about that. Relieved. She'd been so scared that he would reject Ainsley and Peter, but he'd actually done the opposite. He'd embraced them, jumped in full force.

So why did she feel uneasy about it?

She knew why. She was worried he wouldn't stick to his devotion. That he'd prove her right and be discovered as untrustworthy. Of course, Kallie wasn't innocent in this whole situation either, but all the same, she wasn't sure she'd ever fully trust Grant again, no matter what.

Kallie glanced upward again, searching the darkening sky for a moment of clarity. *Lord, help me know what to do now.*

## Chapter Three

The early-morning sun peeked through Grant's broken window shades as he sat on his bed, staring at his laptop. He flipped through photo after photo, pausing on each one, trying to soak in each detail of the precious lives he'd missed.

Last night, he'd called Kallie and asked her to email over as many pictures as she could of the kids, from ultrasounds to this week. She surprised him by saying she already had most of them on a couple of flash drives. He swung by to pick them up, then sat and examined each one into the wee hours. He couldn't bring himself to stop until he'd reached the last photo. And here he was, waking early to look at them again.

His kids. They were perfect. Beautiful. Amazing. His own flesh and blood. So many words and yet none of them quite did Peter and Ainsley justice.

The early pictures were mostly of the kids sleeping, wearing cute outfits that were too big for them. Hard not to be—they were so tiny. Even their skin was too big for them. All those wrinkled rolls on their skinny arms and legs. Grant chuckled, his heart bursting with fierce love and pride he hadn't known was possible.

May 3 was their birthday. What had he been doing last year on that day?

Out of curiosity, he checked his calendar. He'd been preparing for a clinic, about to train a bunch of bird dogs and offer demonstrations in Kansas that coming weekend. Some of his favorite clients. He remembered that whole weekend pretty well, actually.

His kids had been coming into the world at that very moment. How crazy was that?

And how sad. The loss he felt over missing that day, that week in the hospital, and bringing them home ached inside his chest. He had no way of getting those days back. He'd tried to understand. Tried not worrying about it. What was done was done. But why had she kept them from him?

He had to make sure he made the most of every day from now on.

When he reached the final photo again, he shut down his computer and got up for the day. He padded to the kitchen and dug a plastic scoop into the large bag of dog food he'd leaned against a cabinet.

"Chief. Bella."

The dogs scurried in from their sleeping spots in Grant's room, each eagerly awaiting the food as he poured it into their bowls.

He put away the scoop, then reached for the to-do list he'd created last night before calling Kallie about the photos. There was a lot to get done, so he anticipated a very busy day spent contacting people.

At the cottage's tiny, round kitchen table, he perused

his list. Sign up for life insurance and name the kids as beneficiaries. Reroute more of his paycheck to his 401K. Contact Craig Preston, the president of the Helping Hands board, and discuss remote work options.

He paused on the final bulleted task—spend quality time with the kids.

Standing, he left his list on the table before heading out the front door. His stomach growling, he decided another thing to add to his list was to go into Bitter Creek and buy some food to stock his cupboards and fridge. Probably shouldn't raid Kallie's pantry *all* the time.

Chief and Bella were hot on his trail as he strode down the crude road connecting the cottage to Kallie's place. It was really just two dirt tracks worn through the grass by truck tires. Every step filled his mind with memories of working here. Everything from driving the tractor to working dogs to racing over the prairie on a four-wheeler with Kallie sitting behind him, arms holding on tight.

That was where he stopped reminiscing.

Because memories like that couldn't be welcomed anymore. Even though he was back at Bitter Creek Farm for the indefinite future, life wasn't going to return to the way it was back then. His relationship with Kallie wasn't coming back, and he had to learn to be okay with it. Sure, he thought he'd accepted that fact these past two years. But some of those feelings still lingered, and he needed to cut them off before they had a chance to blossom into something detrimental.

He stepped up to Kallie's front door and opened it, placing a soft knock on the frame before entering. "Hello," he called.

Ruby barked twice and hurried to meet him, tail wagging at an exponential speed once she discovered it was someone she recognized.

"Hey, friend." Grant gave her a good rubdown. "I'm happy to see you, too."

When he looked up, he realized Kallie sat at the kitchen table, head in hand, staring at a stack of papers. He waited a couple of seconds, but she didn't move.

"Mornin'," he said.

She popped to life, as if she hadn't noticed him come in. "Oh, hi, sorry. I was just going over Dad's bills."

"Where are the kids?"

"Still sleeping."

Grant glanced at the clock on the stove. "At eight in the morning?"

"I know, it's weird. But I think they're growing. They've been eating a ton and had a long nap yesterday afternoon, too, for Rachel." She got up from her chair and stuck her coffee mug into the microwave.

After approaching the counter, Grant pulled down a mug of his own. He momentarily eyed hers as it turned in circles.

"Do you have to do that very often?" He motioned to the mug. "Reheat your coffee?"

She laughed. "A lot of moms do. I don't even get a chance to make coffee most mornings, so…no, I guess not."

He chuckled and filled his mug, then brought it to his lips. "Mmm, this is good."

"Yeah, when you don't make much of it, you can afford to buy the good stuff."

"Well, prepare to buy the cheap stuff 'cause I drink a lot of coffee."

Kallie's smile faded, then Grant's did, too. The microwave beeped, but she didn't move to open it. Instead, she pushed off the counter and retrieved a plate she'd been using from the table. "Have you eaten? I've got some English muffins in here. Or eggs. Which would you prefer?"

"I'll go light this morning and do a muffin. But I can get it myself." She didn't need to treat him like a guest if he was going to be sticking around. "I'll buy you some more when I go to town today. That business I have to take care of while I'm there? It's for Maxwell Thornton. Do you remember him from high school? He was in the grade above me."

"His little sister was in my class. He's still in town? I thought he moved away."

"Well, I guess he's back. And planning to build a guiding business for bird hunters." Grant stuffed his English muffin into the toaster. "He reached out to me a couple of weeks ago, asking if I had any advice on getting the business up and running. He knew I'd worked with your dad and that his business had a solid reputation. I told him I was going to be passing through on my way to Wyoming, so I'd just stop by. Of course, that was before—"

Before Frank had passed away and Grant had learned the truth.

Kallie frowned. "When do you leave for the clinic?"

"I'm not anymore. It just isn't a great time to be leaving the farm."

Her frown deepened. "Is that going to be okay? Canceling like that? Do you have room to reschedule?"

He hesitated. "My schedule's pretty open right now."

"Why?"

"I canceled them all."

Her brows shot up. "What? You're kidding."

"Look, I want to be here for my kids."

"Grant…" she groaned. "How long are you planning on staying?"

"I told you. I'm not leaving."

"You say that now, but life's going to get in the way. Just watch."

"Why do you assume that?"

"It happens to everyone who tastes freedom. Everyone who has left the farm for a time. Happened to my mom."

"In case you forgot, Kallie, I just found out I was a father less than twenty-four hours ago. It's not fair of you to assume what I will or won't do regarding the kids. And come on. Give me a little credit. I'll stay committed to them."

"Well, you didn't to me."

Grant clamped his jaw shut. *Sorry* didn't even begin to describe how he felt about the way he'd left. Just a month after his proposal, Grant was driving away from Bitter Creek with no plans of returning. It had been stupid, childish. The worst thing he'd ever done. He hadn't known how to deal with anything hard in life.

"I made that mistake once," he said, his voice quiet but strong. "I won't make it again." He'd hoped she would understand but by the wounded look in her eyes, she didn't. "You're just going to have to trust me, Kal."

The toaster popped, so he lifted out his English muffin halves and dropped them onto a plate.

After a few more seconds of silence, Kallie cleared her throat. "So, down to business. If you're going to be living here, then you're going to have to help with the chores."

"I wouldn't have it any other way."

She paused for a moment, as if she'd expected more pushback from him. "Well, good."

Grant took a seat across from Kallie and she immediately leaped from her chair like his muffin had from the toaster. She headed for the living room without a backward glance. "I can't believe the kids aren't awake. They never sleep this long. I'd better check on them."

"Hold up a second."

She stopped in the doorway and slowly turned back.

"I don't want to fight with you all the time," he said.

Maintaining eye contact, she exhaled, as if releasing tension that had been pent up since before he'd arrived. "I don't, either."

"Can't we call a truce or something?"

It took her a long moment to answer, and he wondered what was going through her mind. She never had been much for communication. Which didn't bother Grant, usually—except for when it came to discussing important issues. Like the one they were facing now.

If they weren't going to meet their issues head-on, he'd at least see if they could agree to disagree, rather than watch Kallie sidestep the elephant in the room day after day. He only hoped he could draw out a discussion about their new situation piece by piece, over time.

"Okay," she finally said, finding a faint smile. "A truce it is."

He smiled, too, and hers widened. Man, it was a great smile.

She came back to the table and took a seat, then must have remembered her coffee because she got up to get it.

"I'm glad you brought up chores," Grant began. "I want to split them with you. Sometimes I'll do them, and other times you can. I want a couple of days a week to take care of the kids. To get to know them."

He brought the mug to his mouth, watching her reaction. He could tell she didn't love the idea but thankfully, she nodded. It'd be nice if he could better understand why she had an aversion to him getting involved with the kids. Maybe the truth would come out in time, and maybe he could eventually earn her trust.

"You said you were looking at your dad's bills?"

"Yeah," she said through a sigh, sinking back into her chair and flipping through a couple of pages. "He got a loan at the beginning of this year to pay for the crops. And his combine finally quit a couple summers ago, so he had to get another one. Not to mention all the medical bills." She raised her eyes to meet Grant's. "Dad's savings was next to nothing, and all of these need to be paid off. I just feel all this pressure, like a dragon is breathing down my neck." She rubbed her forehead with both hands and sighed again. "If we can't pay for them, then we'll have to use the estate to do it."

"Now, hold your horses, Kal." Grant sat up so he could lean closer. "I'm sure there's something we can do. How much is the total owed?"

Kallie pointed to a number scribbled on some notebook paper.

Grant tried not to grimace. "Okay, well, it's not as bad as it could be. What about his life insurance policy?"

"Didn't have much. Like, hardly any. He never signed up for one until he found out he was sick." Her expression clouded. "It covered his funeral expenses, but that's about it."

Not good. How sad that Frank had found himself in that situation. Grant couldn't imagine leaving his kids with nothing. Good thing he was inquiring about his own insurance this week. "Don't worry, Kallie. We'll figure it out."

Her shoulders stiffened, and he could almost visibly see the wall going up around her. "Thanks, but it doesn't need to involve you." She bunched all the papers into a tight pile and tapped them together on the table. "I'm the executor of the will, so it's my responsibility."

He drummed his fingers on the table for a moment, debating on how much to say. It might legally be her responsibility, but it was half his estate, too. Not to mention their children's inheritance one day. Finally, he stood, sensing it was time to back off for a bit. "Okay, then. Did you hire a crew to do the spraying?"

"Yep." She didn't look up—kept her gaze fixed on the numbers.

Nodding, Grant headed for the door, his English muffin in hand. "I'm going out to check the fields, then. See what the crew's plans are. I'll be back in a few hours to say hi to the kids."

He glanced behind him, but it was almost like she

hadn't heard him get up. Shaking his head, he pushed open the door and stepped out into the sunlight.

Kallie Shore wasn't used to sharing responsibility. And honestly, why would she be? For two years, she'd been taking care of her dad, the farm and then the twins to boot. But who was caring for her?

Times were changing. She now had a partner in all of this, if only she would realize it.

Kallie took the front steps and headed across the turnaround, zeroing her sights in on the barn. It was naptime, and so with the baby monitor clipped to her pocket, it was time to get some work done.

That work today included starting a garden.

This morning, after she'd figured all of Dad's remaining expenses, she'd lined up all the bills according to size. The best way to build momentum, she figured, was to attack each bill one at a time, smallest to largest. Then she'd jumped on the computer to pay a couple of the really small ones with Dad's savings account.

Now, she was planning out her long game.

There were the crops from her fields, of course, and those would bring in the most money, but not until late in the summer. Until then, she needed other moneymaking options. One of those would be a domestic garden, which she could then harvest for the summer's farmers market in Bitter Creek every Saturday.

And before the garden's harvest was ready, she would bake goods to sell there.

It wasn't going to bring in a ton of money, but it was something. And right now, she'd welcome just about any *something* that came along.

In the barn, she dug through equipment until she reached the tiller. Covered in dust, the dinosaur of a machine hadn't been used since the last time she had a garden—at least two years ago, but possibly three. Now was the time to resurrect the task.

After maneuvering it out of the barn, she pushed the tiller across the turnaround to the large plat where the garden was located. A tall fence surrounded it to keep out animals, and the gate was just wide enough to bring the tiller inside. Working one of these things wasn't easy, and she'd gone soft a little since the kids were born, but if she didn't do it, she'd have to wait and ask Grant to do it whenever he popped back into the house to see the kids.

And she wasn't ready to ask for his help unless she absolutely needed it.

Was it the independent spirit that pushed her to do it on her own? Probably. And the fact that she'd managed the farming business, her dad and two children before this. If she'd lived through that just fine, she could handle a tiller.

Once positioned, she pulled the cord to start it. Nothing happened.

She pulled the cord again. Still nothing.

After some fiddling, it finally jolted to life. Grasping the handles with both hands, she started down one side of the hard, packed earth, turning the soil until it was workable and soft.

The power of the machine's blade pulled it along and rocked the machine as it dug into the ground. Gritting her teeth, Kallie tightened her grip and pushed it forward, willing it to continue the path rather than veer off on its own. The longer she tilled, the softer the ground became beneath her feet and the harder it was to remain steady. Her feet shifted with every step, and her back muscles began to scream at the strain.

Only halfway through, she thought she heard something high-pitched over the grind of the machine's motor. She turned it off, and yep, as the tiller's growl faded away, Ainsley's distinct cry sounded over her baby monitor.

So much for finishing the garden now.

She glanced at the gray clouds hovering in the sky, laden with rain. She didn't know when it would hit, but it sure would be nice to get the garden tilled beforehand. It'd be even nicer to get some of it planted, but that was a wistful dream if she'd ever heard of one.

Leaving the tiller, she headed back to the house.

After getting the kids up, she brought them downstairs to feed them lunch—mashed green beans and cooked sweet potatoes she had on hand in the fridge.

A sudden, distant whir of a motor caught her attention.

"Oh no," she mumbled, heading to the window. She looked out in the direction of the garden, and sure enough, there was Grant. Manhandling that tiller across the rest of the unturned soil. She sighed.

The kids were done eating, so she hoisted them from their chairs and took off across the lawn, a baby on each hip.

The sun, higher now, heated the back of her neck and arms as she approached the high fence. "Grant!" she called, hoping he'd hear her over the tiller.

He glanced at her but continued to turn the soil.

She scrunched her nose. "Grant!"

Peter fussed a little, the noise seeming to bother him. That or the sun—she shouldn't keep the babies out here too long without hats or sunscreen. If only he would stop long enough to listen to her.

Finally, he must have realized she wasn't leaving and cut the tiller's power. He raised his gaze to meet hers.

"I was working on that," she said.

"Yep. And I'm finishing it."

"I was coming back this afternoon."

Grant motioned to the sky. "It'll probably rain by then. Best to get it done now."

Her stomach knotted with guilt. The last thing she'd wanted was to create work for Grant to do. This was her project, her way of helping save Bitter Creek Farm. He wasn't her personal handyman or a hired employee to finish all of her projects for her.

Though, as Grant started up the tiller again and worked his way toward the remaining stretch of dirt, sweat glistening on his neck and seeping through his gray T-shirt, she couldn't ignore the rush of appreciation in her heart. As much as she hated to admit it, it probably would have taken her all afternoon to finish the garden. Time she didn't have, given the impending rainstorm. She definitely had the grit and capability to do it on her own, but a little help from a friend could be welcomed.

And she knew the perfect way to say thank you.

Peter began to fuss again, so she left Grant to the task and took the kids inside.

After she got them interested in some toys on the kitchen floor, she went about collecting supplies to make an apple pie—Grant's favorite dessert. She worked quickly to get it in the oven before Grant finished the garden. And as she finally slipped the pie pan into the preheated oven, the slow rumble of thunder passed over the house.

As she cleaned up the baking supplies and put everything away, she heard Grant cut the tiller's motor. With a glance out the window, Kallie spotted him hauling the machine out of the garden through the gate and then pushing it back to the barn.

More thunder reverberated overhead. Then, the rain came.

The soft patter on the roof of her little home picked up speed, splattering the windowpanes and siding with a steady flow. When Grant emerged from the barn at a run, Kallie hastened to the laundry room just off the kitchen. She yanked a towel from the dryer and darted back to the kitchen as the door opened.

Water soaked Grant's T-shirt and dripped from his hair sticking out from under his ball cap. He met her gaze with an invigorated spark in his eyes and reached for her towel, arms slicked with rain.

"Thanks." He pulled off his cap and tossed it on the nearby counter before scrubbing the towel against his face and arms.

"I still have some of Dad's hooded sweatshirts if you'd like something dry to wear."

"Sure."

Kallie returned to the laundry room and pulled down a box she'd stored on one of the top shelves, full of Dad's old clothing—the stuff she knew he'd loved. She just hadn't had the heart to get rid of those things. A black hooded sweatshirt lay not too deep in the pile, so she pulled it out and brought it to Grant.

He shot her a look of gratitude as he exchanged the towel for the shirt, then headed off for the bathroom.

Ainsley squealed, holding up a bright blue nesting cup she'd successfully pulled out of a purple one.

"Look at you!" Kallie crouched beside her daughter, drinking in her pure sense of accomplishment. "You did it." Gathering some of the cups around her, Kallie slid them into each other and handed them to Ainsley. "So many!"

Giggling, Ainsley grabbed the stacked cups in one pudgy hand, then swiftly turned them upside down, scattering every colored cup across the linoleum. A hardy laugh burst forth from both kids.

"So, I was wonderin' something," Grant said, stepping into the room.

Kallie looked up and stared. Grant looked back at her, Dad's sweatshirt fitting him rather well, and a fresh wave of pain collided with the wall she'd built around her heart. A tsunami of bitter sadness and confusion for why her father, of all people, had been struck down by that horrible disease.

Grant looked down at his shirt and cleared his throat. "It really stinks that he's gone."

She sniffed. "Yeah."

"I miss him, too."

"I know you do."

Grant came in and sat down on the floor next to her, watching the kids play. "I remember once, when I first started working here, he took me out to walk the fields to give the dogs a chance to run. He talked about the loyalty of dogs. It doesn't matter what kind of day you've had or what's going wrong in your life. Your dog is always right there, ready to offer comfort. That's why they're called man's best friend. But even more powerful is God's loyalty. Frank was quick to remind me of that. He told me God could offer more comfort than any dog ever could."

Kallie nodded. "He told me that a lot, too. That, and warned me not to be a hermit all of my life."

Grant chuckled. "Yeah, you could probably hide away for months without coming up for air."

"Pretty much."

"Do you think he left me on the will for a reason?"

The question caught Kallie off guard. The thought had circled into her mind on brief occasions before she'd pushed it away, refusing to consider it. But yeah, what if Dad had left Grant in the will on purpose? What would have been his reasoning? Just so the kids would know their father? Or was there a deeper motivation than that?

Kallie shook her head. "I don't know, Grant. It's impossible to say now."

"Did you know I was still in the will?"

"No, I didn't."

They sat in silence for a moment before Grant shifted his sitting position. "Well, for what it's worth, I'm glad he did. I'm really enjoying getting to know the kids."

She eyed him. "It's only been a day. You stay long enough and I make you do enough farmwork, you might just be singing a different tune."

"Hey, I voluntarily did today's farmwork. And if I could master the tiller, I think I could master most things thrown at me."

Kallie looked away. Time for a change of subject. Conversations like this were good, but if they lasted too long, they deepened to levels she wasn't interested in exploring. "What were you going to say when you first came in? You were wondering something?"

"Oh. Yeah, I was going to tell you I saw Maxwell Thornton today."

"How does his outfit look? His business?"

"Good. I was able to give him a couple of ideas he hadn't thought of yet, and he invited me to come out once the season started."

"That was nice of him."

"Yeah. Anyway, he invited me to his house Sunday night for a birthday thing he's doing for his wife. Said you could come too if you wanted." He angled his head to catch her gaze. "Do you wanna go with me?"

She hesitated. Seemed like an odd way to phrase the situation. Depending on how someone took it, Grant could've meant he'd asked Maxwell if she could come. Or Maxwell could have invited her of his own accord.

"I'm guessing kids can't go," she said.

"Why don't we see if Rachel will watch them?" He smiled. "Come on. When was the last time you had a night out without the kids? Ever?"

He was right—she'd never had a night out since the kids were born. Occasionally she'd asked Rachel to watch them, and that had only been so she could get something else accomplished—like clean the employee's cabin, or meet with Grant about the terms of Dad's will.

It was a night out with Grant, but it would also be

with other people. So maybe it wouldn't be an awkward thing.

"Sure, why not? Sounds fun." She offered a tentative smile.

"Great. And by the way…" Grant sniffed. "Something smells an awful lot like an apple pie. You wouldn't know anything about that, would you?"

"Consider it a thank-you for your hard work on the garden today. And for nearly drowning in the gully-washer afterward."

He broke into a grin, a dimple marking one cheek. "Got any more chores for me to do? I could get used to this kind of gratitude."

Biting back a laugh, Kallie gave his arm a little shove and got to her feet to check the pie.

She glanced back at him as the oven's timer rang out, announcing that the pie was ready. He'd turned his attention to stacking cups with the kids. Earlier, while watching him till the land, she had referred to him in her mind as a friend. And a part of her really missed him as such. Did she dare actually think of him in that way on a more permanent basis?

Maybe Sunday night would give her an answer.

In the nursery, Grant looked about as natural as a horse in a henhouse. But for it being the first time he'd attempted a bedtime routine with babies, he was being a real trouper.

Kallie knelt beside him on the carpeted floor, slipping Ainsley into a fresh pair of footed pajamas after the kids' bath. She couldn't help but glance at Grant's clumsy efforts to put pajamas on Peter, too, while feeling her heart bubble with new respect.

Tonight, he'd fumbled his way through what she was pretty sure was his first diaper change ever. He'd been given a crash course in drawing bathwater and washing hair. And the way he'd played with the kids, like he'd known them for forever?

It was like she wasn't even looking at the same man she'd known a couple years ago. Back then, he'd been young and a little wild, with a head full of big plans. Nothing could tie him down. Had he possibly changed since then?

"You've really hung in there tonight, Grant. Wrangling these peanuts isn't easy."

He caught her eye, the warm glint there unraveling something inside her. "You seem to have it under control."

She chuckled, zipping Ainsley's pink fuzzy jammies up over her bulging baby belly. "You're being very gracious—but thank you."

"I can tell you run a tight ship. That's to be commended." He rolled Peter back toward him as the boy tried to make a break for it.

Kallie grabbed a stuffed animal from a toy bin beside her. "Here."

"Thanks." He handed it over and Peter finally stilled, interested in grabbing the animal's fuzzy ears. "By the way, what's up with these pj's?"

"What do you mean?"

"I mean the zipper's upside down."

Kallie fought a smile. "They zip from the top down—so you can change a diaper without taking the pajamas all the way off. I don't have very many of them, but the ones I have are lifesavers."

"Huh." Grant raised his brows at the pajamas with what looked like new appreciation. "The things they've come up with."

"I know. They've solved problems I didn't even know existed until I experienced them."

Peter tossed his stuffed animal, the toy landing on Ainsley, who scrambled to get up.

"Nice throw, mister." Kallie reached for the animal, only to collide her hand with Grant's, who'd reached for it, too.

He withdrew his hand quickly, animal in his grasp. The soft smile he sent her warmed Kallie clear to her toes.

She lifted Ainsley to put her in her crib and Grant followed close behind. Kallie kissed each child goodnight, and Grant actually managed to make each of them laugh before they turned off the light and left the room.

In the quiet, they made their way downstairs. As they reached the first floor and headed into the kitchen, Grant pulled out his phone and appeared to be checking something.

"Finding anything interesting?" she asked, clearing away dishes from tonight's supper.

"Oh, it's another email from work." He exhaled, the look in his eyes suddenly tired. "I called to tell them the situation, but I only got our secretary, Carol. I had to leave a message with the board president, Craig Preston. Anyway, I told him what's going on, and he just now got back to me."

"About how you can work from home?"

"Well, sort of." Grant shrugged and pocketed his phone. "He's not a fan of my working from here. So I'll have to come up with some good reasons why it would work and present them to him on Monday."

"I see." Kallie busied herself with sticking plates and silverware in the dishwasher, fighting the worry that continued to hound her. Would the strain that staying here was putting on Grant's employment be too much for him to handle? What if he ended up going back to Iowa after all?

She thought about the words Dad had used to describe God's faithfulness, and she tried to apply it to her situation now. No matter how hard things got, He was always there, ready to offer comfort. Some days, she had a hard time believing it. But today, she decided to try her best to lean into it instead.

She only hoped she could see Grant as a friend without getting her heart too attached this time.

## Chapter Four

Getting two babies ready before eight in the morning was like wrestling two octopuses.

"Hold still, Ainsley," Kallie said around a couple ponytail holders caught between her teeth.

She twisted a sprout of her daughter's dark curls around her fingers to secure them while reaching for the comb with her free hand.

Well, free-ish hand. Free when it wasn't redirecting Ainsley back to her lap or batting her puppy stuffed animal out of her face or steadying Peter as he tried to climb into her lap, too, convinced his sister was getting too much of the attention.

Normally, they could go at their leisure. When they worked the fields early, there was no need to fix hair and change out of pajamas. Those things could wait until they came back to the house. But today was Sunday, and Grant would be here soon to accompany them to church. Why he insisted on riding in their car, Kallie didn't know. But regardless, she found herself stressed about getting the kids to look their best for their first time to church with their dad.

But the clock above the TV said he'd be here any minute. She was dragging, slower than usual. It hadn't helped that she'd stayed up way too late, her mind overflowing with worry over Grant and the kids, and so she'd totally slept through her alarm.

Ainsley spotted a toy she wanted and darted forward. Kallie secured the ponytail in the nick of time and let out a whoop, holding up her hands like she'd completed a round of *Celebrity Bake Off.* The little gal still needed a shirt and leggings, but she'd celebrate one success at a time.

"Okay, punkin." She hoisted Peter over her lap and laid him on the carpet. "Time to change your diaper."

And by the smell of things, she was going to need a lot of wipes.

Peter protested being on his back, so she handed him a floppy, stuffed giraffe to keep his interest. She removed the diaper and reached for the wipes...only to find they'd moved several feet away.

"What?" she said under her breath. The package had been right next to her when she'd changed Ainsley. "Peter, don't move."

Holding his legs in one hand, Kallie stretched for the wipes with the other. That's when she spotted Ainsley, barreling toward Peter, squealing with delight and her arms outstretched.

"Oh, no, honey!" Abandoning the wipes, Kallie linked her arm around Ainsley's waist before she could jump on Peter—who promptly wriggled away from Kallie's grasp and took off crawling across the living room floor. Diaperless.

It was then that a knock sounded at the screen door.

Kallie dove after Peter, snatching him before he could get too far. "It's open!"

Soon she heard the screen door open and Grant's shoes crossing the kitchen linoleum. "Kallie?"

"In here." As he appeared around the corner, she placed Peter back on the carpet in their starting position. "Could you grab that package of wipes by your feet?"

"Oh, sure." He scooped up the package and opened it as he passed it off.

"Thanks." She slipped out a wipe, sending him a quick smile.

Which nearly made her do a double take. Grant stood there in a blue Western shirt with pearl snaps and, again, sleeves rolled to the elbows. His signature look. One that used to make her go weak at the knees. Might still have that power if she wasn't careful.

"Can I help you with anything?" Grant stepped farther into the room—gingerly, as it was littered with two nursing pillows, the kids' car seat carriers, this morning's jammies and the day's clothes. Toys, so many toys. And clean diapers Ainsley had successfully pulled out of the caddy Kallie had refilled last night. So much for wanting everything to be perfect.

She tossed him Peter's pants and shirt, then secured the fresh diaper on her son. "Can you put these on Peter, please?" She released him and snagged Ainsley as she toddled by, a container of diaper rash ointment in her chubby hand.

Kallie removed the ointment from her daughter's

possession and slipped her leggings up over her legs. "Pants," she announced to Ainsley. "They go on your legs." She wasn't sure how much the kids actually understood at this age, but the internet said to talk to babies constantly about what you were doing.

"Did I get the time wrong, or are we supposed to be out the door in ten minutes?" Grant asked.

"Yes, if we want to be on time." Which she knew he did. "Sorry, I'm running behind."

"No worries. Glad I could help."

She glanced at him. Peter squirmed as the shirt was pulled over his head at a rather slow, awkward speed. If she wasn't mistaken, uncertainty flickered in Grant's eyes as he fumbled with Peter's flailing arms.

"Any experience changing kids' clothes?" she asked.

"Um…that would be a no."

His tone sounded sheepish, which made her feel a little guilty for asking. "Sorry, I didn't mean anything by it. Peter's resilient. It won't hurt him if it takes a bit to put on his shirt and pants."

With the apology hanging between them, both went back to dressing the kids. Still, the sting was there, behind it all. The reminder that Grant was their father by blood but hadn't been around for any of their upbringing. Not knowing about them was Kallie's fault. But if he'd known, would he have come around, what with his thriving businesses and aversion to fatherhood? Or had he needed to be here for the inheritance in order to connect with the kids and make the leap to stay?

And which was worse for the kids—growing up with a dad who never knew they existed or one who just chose to stay away?

They loaded the kids and bags into Kallie's extended cab truck. She gave Grant a quick lesson in how to harness the babies in their car seats before shuffling a few items to make room for the diaper bag, a toy bag to keep the kids occupied during the service and a picnic lunch for afterward.

Finally, they were off.

It felt odd being in the driver's seat while Grant sat beside her. When they'd dated, it had always been the other way around. But Kallie quickly shook the thought from her mind and focused on the gravel road. All memories from their dating days should be held at bay. Because he might say he was determined to stick around for the long haul, but she'd seen firsthand how restless he got during the long hours of harvesting, stuck inside a combine, and that time wasn't far off. So it didn't matter what the past was like—what mattered was keeping her head now.

"I thought we'd have a picnic lunch after church," she said, purposefully changing the course of her thoughts. "That little park near the church would be perfect. It's so nice right now, and I'd like to get the kids outside before it gets too hot to do these kinds of outings."

"Good idea."

She glanced in Grant's direction, but he had his gaze trained on the surrounding prairie, his knee bouncing to the beat of the country song on the radio. She waited a few more seconds, but he offered no further thoughts.

Suppressing a sigh, she worked her grip on the steering wheel, telling herself that it was better if they didn't connect again like they had last night. Better to stay platonic partners only.

She stopped the pickup at the end of the gravel road, waiting until a car passed so she could get onto the highway that led to Bitter Creek. While they sat there, her cell phone's ringtone sprang to life.

Who was calling on a Sunday morning?

She glanced at her phone before exhaling and dropping it onto the middle of the bench seat.

"Who is it, a telemarketer?"

"No. My mom." Kallie eased onto the gas pedal, making her way onto the highway.

"Aren't you going to answer it?"

"I think she's just wondering if she got any more of Dad's money in his will."

Grant was silent a moment as the ringtone finally died away. "Did she tell you she was?"

"No." She'd received some already—it'd been Dad's personal choice to offer it, since they were divorced. "But I don't know why else she'd call."

Grant shrugged. "I mean, you *could* answer it..."

She shot him a glare. "It's not as easy as answering a simple phone call. It's—it's managing the door of communication that would open as a result." She'd have to brace herself against the excuses that would only serve to hurt her.

An incoming text chimed.

Out of the corner of her eye, she could tell Grant was watching her. Then he tipped his head a bit to see her screen.

"She says she has something important to discuss with you."

She shrugged. "I guess she'll just have to wait until

sometime when I'm free. Like after the kids graduate college."

Grant chuckled under his breath. "Come on, Kallie. What do you have against your mom that you won't even call her back?"

"Would you call your dad back if he called?"

"That's different."

"Is it?" Her shoulders felt rigid beneath the weight of this discussion. She threw him a quick look. "To answer your question, when you worked here, how often did my mom come home?"

"Just once. For your graduation. But your parents split sometime around then, I think."

"Yeah. Once. She missed everything."

"But that was years ago."

"Yes. That doesn't mean time has healed anything, though. And like I said, you of all people should know what it's like to grow up with a difficult parent."

Grant cleared his throat. "My dad finds excuses not to work, and your mom is one of the most ambitious people I can think of. I don't think that's the same thing."

"It's *totally* the same thing. I mean, yes, she was here for the ceremony, but not the work leading up to it. While other moms were sending out graduation party invitations and scooping watermelon balls into a serving bowl and deciding what kind of punch to make, mine was off closing deals."

Grant frowned. "That's a little harsh, isn't it?"

Kallie didn't answer at first. "Maybe. But whenever she came home, she always wanted to act like no time had passed, that we were still okay. But the truth was, we hardly knew each other." She shook her head. "It's not supposed to be that way with your mom."

"Do you think she might want to heal things?"

Thickness gathered in her throat. "If that's the case, then she should've come to Dad's funeral."

Kallie thought about her mother throughout church services while Grant stood beside her and sang, his baritone so familiar. She knew she was being prickly, and she wished she wasn't. But how did someone move past hurt that ran so deep? She wished she knew.

Ainsley bounced on Grant's lap during the church service, her curls dancing as she waved her doll back and forth in front of her. Apparently the way the doll's frilly dress and yarn hair swayed with each movement fascinated her.

And it made Grant smile. Beam with pride, really, to fully be in his kids' lives. The only thing that would make it better was if Kallie would relax into this new situation they'd been handed. He wasn't asking for her to love him again. He wasn't even asking her to like him. He knew that ship had sailed. But it would be nice to be considered an equal—in parenting and in running the farm.

After services ended, the quiet din of congregants rose around them. It was a pretty small church, as Bitter Creek itself was tiny, and he was fairly certain they all knew he was the twins' dad. For him, attending church was important regardless of how people felt about him, so he'd come anyway. But he'd fully expected to defend to people why he was back in town.

Surprisingly, though, no one asked. Several old

friends turned to greet him, and they seemed genuinely happy to see him there.

"Huh. Interesting," he murmured as the last person headed away.

"What'd you say?" Kallie looked up from strapping Peter into his car seat carrier on the pew beside Grant.

"Nothing." He smiled in response. "Just happy to be back."

A very brief shadow crossed her gaze before she returned his smile. Then her gaze focused on something behind him, and she straightened.

"Grant Young."

He turned, finding Brendan Millard standing behind them.

"Hey there, Brendan." Grant reached out to shake the man's hand, spotting his cousin Ronnie Millard closing in, as well.

Brendan stared at Grant for a second, long enough to size him up, before finally sliding his hand into Grant's. "Didn't expect to find you here."

Ronnie popped up beside Brendan, small in frame for a man, though he held his chin up as if wanting to appear bigger.

"Yeah. Got in last week. You'll be seeing a lot more of me around here now, helping with the farm and the kids." Grant turned a hand to the cousin. "Mornin', Ronnie."

Ronnie gave him a quick nod, almost not offering a handshake until he glanced around, probably thinking about appearances.

Kallie reached for Ainsley, then scrunched her nose. "Oops. Seems like she needs a diaper change before we go. Excuse me." She slipped out of the pew, leaving Grant with the guys.

He sent Peter a smile and a wave, the boy giggling in return from his seat.

"So, you leave suddenly, and then Kallie lets you come back?"

There was the question he'd been expecting. "I own part of the farm now, since Frank passed away."

"Oh." Brendan glanced at his cousin, who mirrored his face as his brows arched high. "Seems strange. You getting part of the farm."

"Hey now." Grant frowned. "I'm not about to discuss what Frank's intentions were. I'm simply honoring the man's wishes."

"And stepping into Kallie's family."

He knew Millard didn't like him, but that was apparently an understatement.

Before he could answer, Kallie was standing beside him. "And he's been a huge help."

Grant wanted to shoot her a glance, but he kept his eyes fixed on Brendan. Was she sticking up for him?

Brendan lifted a brow. "Is he?"

"I just offer help where I can. But Kallie's a great mom. She doesn't need anyone's help. She's fully capable. I'm just here for support and getting to know my kids."

"We'd better go," Kallie added. "The kids are going to get hungry if we wait too long."

"Right you are." He lifted his cowboy hat from the pew and placed it on his head. "See you around, folks."

"Bye." Kallie tossed their visitors a smile before turning it on Grant. Was it just him or did her eyes soften when she looked at him? They shuffled out of the pew, each with a car seat carrier in tow. Once they reached the church entryway, she turned to him. "I got Rachel to watch the kids for us tonight—during the party."

He brightened and leaned a palm on the door handle to let Kallie outside. "Great. We'll drop them off on the way."

As she exited the church, she suddenly stopped and he nearly bumped into her. She faced him, her eyes looking soft again. "Thank you for what you said to Brendan. About me, and about Dad."

"You heard even the part about your dad?"

"Ainsley's diaper emergency ended up being a false alarm. I was on my way back."

Chuckling, Grant followed her out into the sunlight. It was turning out to be a hot one—which was good, because that probably meant the temperature would linger into the evening some, keeping Maxwell Thornton's outdoor party comfortable. He hadn't been particularly interested in the get-together when the guy first mentioned it, but after he said Grant could bring someone along, it had given him the idea to invite Kallie. She was doing an excellent job of taking care of the kids, but he continued to think about the fact that no one took care of her, too.

This was his way of helping out. If it gave her a moment to relax, then he'd be happy. If it helped them become equals—maybe even friends—he'd be more than happy.

"Okay." Kallie reviewed the numbers on the paperwork in her lap. "I've depleted Dad's savings and posted a few things for sale online. Then there's the garden that'll start producing later this summer, and any baking I can get done—"

"Yes. Pies. You should definitely make more of those and sell them. But maybe keep a few at home for me." Grant gave her a wink before returning his focus to the road.

She laughed. "Okay, we'll see what I have time for. Any other ideas?" She scratched her head as they entered Bitter Creek. "Maybe I should get a part-time job. One I can work from home."

"What? No." Grant's eyes met hers. "You're busy enough as it is with the farm and the kids."

"But the money—"

"We'll find it another way, don't worry."

She sent him a look and he must have been able to interpret it.

"Look, Kal. I watched my mom work two, sometimes three jobs to make ends meet because my dad couldn't hold down even one. If anyone has to get a second job, it'll be me. You've already got a lot on your plate."

She did. There was no denying it even though she wanted to.

Evening light cast a soft glow over the prairie landscape, and an exhilarating thrill skittered over her. Not that this was a date, but it sort of resembled one, and she hadn't been on one in years.

"Also," he added, "I have a little savings I can dip into."

Thoughts of a date skidded to a halt. "No, Grant, really. I can't let you do that—"

"You can if you want to keep the farm. Besides, this is my home, too, now, remember? And the kids' inheritance one day."

She stared at him for a few second before relaxing her shoulders and looking out the window. "Well, thank you."

The one street lamp in town popped on, and Grant turned the corner just before Rachel's house. "Hmm."

"What?"

"Oh, nothing. I just thought I would have gotten more pushback from you, that's all." He eyed her with a spark that had her fighting back a smile.

"I figured you needed a win every now and then."

"I appreciate that."

They parked outside Rachel's house and dropped off the kids before being on their way to Maxwell Thornton's party. He was holding it at his house in their backyard, and Grant had said it was "a small shindig," but when they arrived and had to park down the street behind a whole bunch of other vehicles, Kallie was fairly certain it was anything but.

They strolled down the sidewalk past a couple of houses until they reached the right one—a modest house like many others in Bitter Creek, with whitewashed siding and cute black shutters. Rosebushes in the flower beds and an apple tree near the front walk.

In the backyard, string lights swooped from pole to pole in a whimsical web of stars, and mellow acoustic music played over a speaker somewhere. A couple of long folding tables had been set up along one side of the yard, draped in white tablecloth with scores of desserts and finger-food appetizers. A firepit in the yard's center boasted short, upturned logs for chairs and what looked like a decorated umbrella stand full of thin sticks. The sign hanging from the stand said "For S'mores."

Even the lawn games and a photo booth set up in another corner of the yard were charming.

Kallie couldn't help but feel a hint of excitement. "Okay. This is going to be cool."

"I guess, if you like this sort of thing."

She sent him a knowing smile. Grant wasn't much for charm and sentiment. All that romantic stuff—it just wasn't his thing. But that wouldn't stop her from enjoying herself tonight.

Right off the bat, she dragged him to the photo booth. She stuck a funny hat on his head and she wore a feather boa and sunglasses while the camera snapped away. Every time Grant shot her an annoyed look, she couldn't help but grin in response. Which generally made him crack a smile, too.

Eventually, after chatting with some old friends, meeting a few new ones and sampling a little bit of everything from the refreshment table, Kallie and Grant wound up at the firepit. A few others had gathered there as well, the night air tinged with a slight chill on the breeze.

Kallie turned the thoughts in her mind to the same speed as her marshmallow over the flames. "If you could visit anywhere in the world, where would it be?"

Grant shrugged. "I guess maybe it'd be cool to see the ocean. But I've really enjoyed traveling the country with my clinics, and I'm not sure there's anywhere else I want to see." He pulled his marshmallow from the fire, blackened the way he liked it. "What about you?"

"When I was in eighth grade, I did a genealogy project and learned my family came through Ellis Island. There's a book they have on display with everyone's names. Since then, I thought it would be really cool to go." She pulled her marshmallow out of the flames and lightly squeezed it. Nope, still firm. Gingerly, she placed it back near the fire and began to rotate her stick. "Dad couldn't go with me, with the farm and dog training keeping him so busy."

Grant sat so close, his arm brushed against hers as he regarded her. "And your mom?"

"She said she'd take me but it never happened." She shrugged it off, then plucked her marshmallow from the fire. If it wasn't done by now, she'd just eat it the way it was.

"At least both your parents were interested in doing fun things with you," Grant said. "My mom was, but she worked too much. Dad was always available but never had the time, if that makes sense." He stared into the fire as it crackled and popped embers into the dark sky. "There was one time I remember where he actually acted interested in hanging out with us. Together, we walked around the neighborhood doing a paper route of sorts. We didn't know anything at the time. All we knew was that we got to spend time with Dad like other kids got to do with theirs."

"How old were you?"

"Seven. So Jill was nine," he said. "Anyway, sometimes the people we gave papers to would give my dad money. Sometimes it was dark bottles, though we had no idea what they were."

Kallie arched her brows. "They paid him in alcohol?"

"Yeah, I guess so. Then he disappeared into some guy's house for—well, I don't know for how long, but it was a good, long while. I still don't know what they were doing in there, but here we were, two little kids, stuck in the front yard of some run-down house in a trashy neighborhood." Grant shook his head. "We could've been hurt. Or worse. My dad was careless. He only thought about himself."

"And you were only seven?"

"Yep."

"I'm sorry he did that to you, Grant. That's crazy." Her heart hurt for kids that had to live through childhoods like that. She'd been missing her mom, certainly, but neither of her parents had ever put her in danger. "I didn't know about all that."

Grant scrunched his nose. "I don't talk about it much." As if to change the subject, he grabbed another marshmallow. "How about a contest? Let's see who can roast the most perfect marshmallow."

"According to whose standards?"

"Yours. No black marks, no charring, no smoke damage. Just a rich, plump, golden brown." Grant tossed a marshmallow to Kallie, then stuck his own on his stick. "Ready? And go!"

Monday night, moonlight cast leafy shadows across Kallie's house as Grant stood beneath the old tree in the front yard. Light glowed through the kitchen window's curtain, and his stomach rumbled in anticipation. After working all day on random farm chores and beginning to fix up the cottage, he was looking forward to a big home-cooked meal tonight.

Back in Iowa, home cooked meant macaroni and cheese out of a box. But unlike him, Kallie knew how to cook. That, and seeing Ainsley and Peter, had kept his steps incredibly light throughout the day.

As did the memory of spending last night around the fire with Kallie, just like old times. He hadn't sat around a campfire probably since they'd dated, and the sound of crackling wood and the spray of ember fireflies had taken him back there in a blink.

Which was obviously messing with his mind—making him want to do ridiculous things like put on aftershave and a nicer shirt after showering before coming over here. Must have inhaled too much wood smoke.

Smoothing back his unruly hair, Grant strode up the front walk. The phone in his back pocket chimed—must've picked up Kallie's Wi-Fi—so he paused to check the new email message. It was a reply from the life insurance company he'd written to last week. Looked like in order to qualify, he needed to get on the phone for a lengthy interview about his life history. Something that had to be done during normal business hours. Maybe he could do it tomorrow, if Kallie agreed to let him watch the kids for the day while she worked the farm.

Grant slid his phone back in his pocket and opened the screen door.

Ruby let out a sharp bark from right inside, no doubt guarding the place from intruders. Grant quickly slid to his knees and buried his fingers in her copper ears and in the ticking along her neck and shoulders.

"Good girl," he murmured. "It's just me."

A baby's soft whimper carried in from the living

room, and suddenly Grant realized no one was in the kitchen with him. No supper smells lingered in the air, either. He stood, frowning. Was everything okay? Had Kallie forgotten about their plan for tonight?

He made his way into the living room and found her—sunk into the overstuffed recliner, a sleeping baby nestled in each arm.

She looked up, eyes tired, offering a half smile. "They've been cranky all afternoon and finally fell asleep. I didn't have the heart to move."

Seeing her like this, with the twins cuddling against her and breathing deeply, made something thicken in his chest. Brought his emotions a little closer to the surface than he wanted them to be.

He had to snap out of it. Blinking, he broke the stare. "Did I hear one of them crying just now?"

"Ainsley startled at Ruby's bark, but it didn't fully wake her…as you can see." Laughing softly, she lowered her gaze to her daughter, whose tiny thumb had taken refuge in her mouth.

Kallie's glow of admiration was nearly palpable, overcoming Grant to the point that he couldn't ignore it anymore. There was something truly special about being a parent, and he longed to *really* know what it felt like. Lifting one corner of his mouth, he knelt beside the recliner and swept his gaze over each child, in awe of the peace resting across their cherub faces.

"They're something else, aren't they?" He nearly reached out to touch Peter's shoulder, clothed in green and grey stripes, but stopped himself for fear of waking him.

Kallie released a sigh. "They are."

He could hear her fatigue even as she tried to hide it. He'd never taken care of kids this little, especially not two of them, so he couldn't imagine how much work they were. Though anything done on your own for too long could feel exhausting.

He stood. "Are you hungry? Let me make something for you."

"Oh, really, Grant. You don't need to."

"It's no problem." He stood before she could stop him. "I'll look in the fridge and see what's there."

"You won't find much," he heard her mumble, probably more to herself than to him.

She was right. When Grant opened the fridge and inspected its contents, he found the farm usuals—butter, eggs, milk, but nothing substantial. There was always an omelet, he supposed.

He opened the freezer. Bingo. Frozen pizza. Just his style.

After pulling out the flat box, he stuck his head back into the living room. "How does pepperoni and sausage pizza sound?"

Kallie's eyes lit. "Perfect, actually."

Grant set the oven temperature and readied the pizza to bake. As he did, he heard one of the kids fuss a little, though not for long. Apparently Kallie was pretty good at soothing them. Which baby had cried, Grant had no idea. But one day, he would know who was who just by their sound.

Growing up, there'd been times he'd gone a week without his dad saying a word to him. If Grant had left town for a few nights, he suspected the man hadn't even known he'd been gone. While his dad lay on the couch,

Mom had worked two jobs and still made it to many of Grant's school activities. His father's absence had stung for a while, but eventually Grant had numbed himself to the pain. However, having kids of his own brought a lot of that pain back to the surface—and made him realize he hadn't actually coped with any of those emotions.

He never wanted to put his kids through something like that—the possibility of messing up really made him nervous.

Leaving the oven to preheat, he returned to the living room. Kallie looked up from the sleeping babies.

"Have you thought any more about me watching the kids tomorrow?" he asked. "I'd like to."

She nodded, lips pressed together as if she'd given it a lot of thought. "I think that's a good idea. It'll give them a chance to get to know you…and for you to know them."

"That's what I was thinking, too. Maybe tonight after they go to sleep, you can show me what's what around here."

"Deal."

In his opinion, she looked a little uncertain about the whole thing, but he didn't need her to be fully convinced. Just needed her to let go of enough control to give him a chance.

The oven chimed, so he went back into the kitchen to put in the pizza.

But before he could put the pizza in, he heard one of the babies start to fuss. The baby's cries grew louder. He hastened back into the living room.

It was Peter.

The boy's fussing had grown into restless fidgets.

Kallie shifted to accommodate him, but if he rolled too much more, he'd wake Ainsley.

"Can I take him?" Grant stepped forward.

"Please."

He gently scooped up his son and headed for the kitchen. "You hungry, bud?" In the doorway, he looked back at Kallie, who'd settled back in order to keep Ainsley sleeping. "What can I feed him?"

"You can start with a bottle."

A bottle. Yes. He could do that. It wasn't hard, right?

Entering the kitchen, he looked around. Now, if he were a bottle, where would he be? He could ask Kallie. Or he could look for it himself and save her the headache of explaining everything. Scanning the counter proved fruitless, so he zeroed in on the cabinets.

Peter, sucking a pacifier, quietly watched what Grant did through sleep-puffed eyes. Grant crouched to check inside a bottom cabinet but had to stop to balance Peter, who apparently hadn't figured out how to hold on yet or grip his legs around Grant's torso. Something he figured every baby knew how to do instinctively. Guess it was learned.

Finally, he located the bottles in an upper cabinet, and thankfully, a tub of formula sat beside them. He pulled each out and inspected the back of the container for directions. Mix with water. Okay, not so hard. He took the lid off his chosen bottle and raised his brows at its inner workings. Weren't bottles supposed to be a lid and a cup it screwed onto? What was all this extra complex stuff?

The pizza. He'd forgotten to put it in. Mindful of Peter, he held tightly to his son while he opened the oven door and slid the pizza pan inside. After setting the timer, he returned to the bottle.

He filled it as directed, and as he shook it, Peter whimpered and reached for it. "Smart kid," he murmured with a smile. "You recognize this, don't you?"

Shaking it in his free hand, he headed back into the living room and took a seat on the sofa. As gently as he could, he laid Peter back against the crook of his arm and put the bottle in his mouth.

Peter grappled for the bottle, pushing his tiny fingers through Grant's to get a grip.

"He can hold it by himself," Kallie said softly. "In fact, he'd prefer to."

Grant moved out of Peter's way, and Peter went to town on that bottle. One-handed. "Well, I'll be. What a rock star."

Just then, Ainsley rolled and stretched, opening her eyes. Her hair was everywhere—curls that couldn't be tamed. Kallie stood and took her into the kitchen, probably to get her a bottle, too.

When the buzzer sounded again. Grant made eye contact with Peter over the bottle. "Well, that was fast."

He beelined to the kitchen to find Kallie turning off the oven.

"Nope, let me get it." Grant beat her to a drawer and pulled out a pot holder.

"No, it's fine, I—"

"I told you I'd make you supper," Grant reminded, opening the oven door, "and that's exactly what I'm going to do."

He set Peter in his high chair so he could use both hands to steady the steaming pizza and shut the oven door. Quickly, he sliced it and took down a couple of plates.

He glanced at Kallie, who stood there watching him as if she was shocked to see him preparing food. "Go sit," he told her. "Peter and I are right behind you."

Without saying anything, she retreated.

When he joined her, she had settled back into her recliner with a bottle for Ainsley. He handed her a plate and sat with his, allowing Peter to lay with his bottle across Grant's lap.

Kallie took a bite and nodded. "Yep. Hits the spot. Thanks for making this."

"No problem."

"It's probably the best pizza I've ever had—because someone else made it."

Grant chuckled before eating another bite. "Well, I've learned a thing or two about preparing food since I've been on my own. Literally only a thing or two, but it's more than I knew before I left home."

Kallie laughed. And when she did, it lifted a weight off his chest he hadn't even known was there. It was like they were really at a truce and that it was actually possible to make this thing work.

But his thoughts were interrupted when Peter threw his empty bottle and cried out in what appeared to be frustration.

"Your milk all gone, bud?" Grant stooped to retrieve the bottle. "Are you still hungry?" He glanced at Kallie in question.

"There's baby food in the freezer." She started to move, but Grant stood first.

"I'll get it. Stay and eat." She already served the kids

every day with unswerving devotion. He could earn his own keep around here.

She shot him a grateful look and sat back. "They're frozen in the shape of ice cubes and separated by food type in freezer bags. Pick a few cubes of any flavor you'd like and put them in a small pot on the stove until they melt."

Okay, easy. He moved into the kitchen and did that very thing, choosing cubes of butternut squash and heating them on the stove. Peter watched with complete interest from Grant's arm.

"Grant?" Kallie's voice drifted in.

"Yeah?"

"Might as well put on a few more cubes for Ainsley, too."

"Consider it done." He returned to the freezer to grab more. "Genius idea, these frozen cubes of baby food," he called out to her.

"You can thank the internet."

"Easy to store and all organized. With labels and dates, too. You sure have things under control around here." It was impressive to say the least—internet or not.

Grant fought against the feelings of doubt, stirring the cubes as they melted into a soupy consistency. She'd done completely fine without him this whole time. What could he possibly add to this family that she hadn't already provided? Besides his 401k and life insurance. And willing his half of the estate to her and the kids so it would always stay in the family.

No matter how he looked at it, his only contribution here was providing for the future—nothing for here and now.

And Jill was right—Kallie was a tough and independent woman. It had him nervous. What if he was
wasting his time trying to break his way into the kids'—
and Kallie's—lives? Sure, she'd let him make supper
tonight. Barely. But what about other responsibilities?
Tomorrow, next week, next month, in a year? Would
she eventually edge him out of the picture?

# *Chapter Five*

❧

Things were looking up. Through the paternity test results, Grant had received confirmation that he was indeed Peter and Ainsley's biological dad. And now, he was about to get his life insurance sorted out.

"All right, we should be good to go." The chipper middle-aged nurse named Liza packed up the paperwork and other materials into her travel bag. She offered Grant a smile as she stood up from Kallie's kitchen table. "We'll send this blood work and everything in, and the life insurance company will be in contact with you soon, okay?"

"Sounds great," Grant replied, standing, too. "Thanks for coming."

Kallie was out getting farm chores done for most of the day, so he'd spent it with the kids. The kids had fallen asleep at the normal time for their nap, just after the nurse showed up to give him his medical screening, which he discovered was a requirement to be approved for life insurance. He'd had to excuse himself to take the kids upstairs, but not before Peter and Ainsley, tired yet charming, had made friends with Liza.

Now, the nurse headed for the door. "Thanks for letting me interrupt your busy day. Looks like you have your hands full."

Grant glanced at the dirty dishes in the sink, and the colorful kid plates still sitting on the kids' high chair trays. And the laundry basket overflowing in the living room and the smattering of toys across the kitchen, where the kids had been playing while Grant tried to get work done on his laptop.

"You've only seen half of it," he mumbled.

He held the door open for her as she chortled. "My niece has twins. They're three, and are they ever busy." She pointed to the ceiling with her pen, likely indicating the kids upstairs. "But these ones are cuties. Better watch your girl in high school. Just joking—but it'll be here before you know it. You're doing a great job, seem like a great dad. I can tell how much they love you." Winking, Liza headed out onto the porch and then down the steps. "Have a great day."

"Thanks," he called back, his heartbeat banging around in his chest.

Sure would be nice if he was actually the dad she claimed he was. But he recognized empty flattery disguised as small talk when he saw it. It might be a while before Ainsley or Peter really bonded with him, but hopefully it would be before high school.

High school. That seemed like a world away, considering they were only thirteen months old. Then again, the past two years had flown by, so Liza was probably right. Was he prepared to raise these kiddos for the next seventeen years or more? Could he learn to be okay with living on the farm that long and coparenting with Kallie all that time without knowing if he was truly contributing anything?

Suddenly, he heard one of the kids crying in their room. Grant cut his gaze to the sound and frowned. Then he checked the clock. Just as he thought. It'd only been half an hour. Weren't they supposed to sleep longer than that?

He stood and crossed the linoleum. It wasn't long before the second baby joined in.

But as his feet clomped up the stairs, the crying died away and fits of laughter filtered down from the nursery instead. He paused outside the nursery door, listening to the innocent, from-the-belly laughter while his chest expanded with pride.

Didn't matter how many baskets of laundry there were. Or meals to make or toys to clean up. If this was going to be the rest of his life, he'd take it in a heartbeat.

If only he knew what his purpose here was—how he could contribute and make a difference.

Which was what made the separation from his job at Helping Hands so difficult right now. He really enjoyed his position there as executive director. It was deeply fulfilling work where he was making a noticeable impact in the lives of dogs and their new owners. The success was measurable. Easy to calculate as solid proof whenever he faced a challenging week. But parenting? Apparently there weren't very many hard and fast indicators of success. He pretty much felt like he was throwing spaghetti at the wall each day. Not a position he found very comfortable.

He opened the nursery door, revealing the twins standing face-to-face where their cribs butted together, no doubt thoroughly enjoying each other's company. Their laughter stopped at the sound of the door opening, but their faces brightened again at the sight of Grant.

Ainsley squealed. "Ma-ma-ma!" She bounced, chubby hands banging against the crib railing.

"No, little miss. Daddy. I'm Daddy." He approached their cribs, and they beamed up at him. "Daddy!"

Peter began to laugh.

"You can say it. Dad-dy. Daddy. *Dad-dy.*" He sounded it out carefully for them.

Now they both stared at him like he'd lost his mind. Awesome.

Grant sighed and scooped the kids up, one in each arm. "Never mind. We'll work on it again another time."

As they headed down the stairs to the living room, another email chimed on his phone. It'd been going off nearly constantly today, between work commitments and the movers he'd hired to bring all of his stuff here from Iowa—everything except his 1952 Mercedes-Benz 220 Cabriolet, which he'd restored and now kept in storage until he could figure out the best way to get it out here.

Ah, that Mercedes. He still couldn't believe the unbelievable deal he'd got on it from his buddy. He'd actually tried convincing his friend to sell it for more, but bottom line, his friend just wanted it out of his garage. He'd inherited it years ago from an elderly uncle he hadn't known well, and he himself wasn't into restoring cars. Not that Grant had been much, either—but he knew a looker when he saw it.

In Cedar Falls, Iowa, he'd lived inside the city in a cramped apartment with only one parking spot, where he'd kept his beat-up truck, which he also loved, like a worn-in shoe. Now though, living out here on the South Dakota prairie, he could imagine driving that Mercedes down the highway, with the warm breeze rushing over him with the top down and the cherry-red exterior gleaming in the sunlight.

He got Peter and Ainsley interested in some toys before sliding the phone from his pocket.

Will Parker, wanting him to call ASAP.

Grant glanced in the kitchen at the phone hanging on the wall a foot from him. He hated using her land-line all the time, but it was pretty much the only option. He'd offer to pay her bill this month. Focusing on what Will might be calling about, he picked up the receiver, punched in the number and wedged it between his ear and shoulder.

"Hello?"

"Hey, Will, it's Grant. Using a landline. What's up?"

"We had our meeting last night."

Grant's ears perked up. Well, that was certainly a step forward. "Great. How'd it go?"

"Well, we brought on some new sponsors. One of them—the one donating the most, actually—has more specifications he'd like hammered out before he'll supply any money for the rebuild."

"What kind of specifications?" Will and everyone else on the board had been pretty secretive about the previous specifications, information which he still hadn't really been given access to.

Craig Preston, the board president, met with sponsors on a regular basis, but generally they weren't major, and generally, they didn't want to dip their fingers into the inner workings of Helping Hands.

Hopefully Will would help Grant out here with some information. "Come on. What does he want to do?"

"Well…" The board contact exhaled. "The biggest thing is widening the parameters of who can adopt a dog."

Grant frowned, glancing quickly at Peter and Ainsley, who were each captivated with whatever various toys they'd discovered. "I don't know if I like that, Will. The qualifications are narrow for a reason. It's our responsibility to put setters into homes that are well-suited to them."

"I know. We'll be putting it to a vote at our next meeting."

Next meeting? "When's that?"

"We're holding a special one in two weeks."

At least that was good news—they generally only scheduled one every few months. "What else does the guy want?"

Will seemed to hesitate. "He wants to limit foster care homes and rebuild the facility with kennels."

Grant straightened. "Like a traditional animal shelter?"

"Yeah. He figures it'll cut down on transportation costs and keep all dogs readily available for screening and adoptions. Probably less paperwork. And less confusion on where every dog is—all that kind of stuff."

He wanted to scoff. "Yeah, but putting setters in a home situation helps them adapt quicker to their new way of life. It gives us an opportunity to truly evaluate their temperaments and needs, and match them with the right home. You know all that."

Will sighed. "Yeah, I know. But you know the hassle of trying to maintain a foster home list, too."

Yeah, that was definitely true. It wasn't easy keeping foster families. They'd made it a policy to generally only place one dog per household, at least at first. And very rarely with a family that already had a dog living there—which meant that any foster family who adopted the dog they housed might not be able to foster again. All of that significantly reduced their options. Grant spent countless hours each month calling and searching for more families to fill in the gaps. It was a stressful, long and tedious process.

But was Will actually advocating for this sponsor's specifications?

"Parker, I'm not a fan," Grant said. "I've got some big problems with these ideas."

"I figured you would," Will replied. "That's why I think you should come back so we all can discuss it in person—before the meeting solidifies things."

Grant glanced at the kids, reminded of his promise to Kallie. "I don't think I can make it in the next two weeks. Can I teleconference?"

He was trying his best—he'd been working from his laptop in the late evenings and during the kids' naps on the days he watched them. It was important not to disappoint Kallie. She needed to trust him before he left the state, and he highly suspected it would take him longer than a couple weeks to earn it.

"We need you to be here," Will said. "We've been

understanding that you needed the week to get your affairs in order, but any longer than that is pushing it."

"Will, I told Craig about my situation out here, how it's changed. I need some time to figure things out."

"Man, honestly, I'm being more up front with you than Craig will be, but we're all feeling the strain here at Helping Hands. You need to come back so we can discuss this."

Grant swallowed. Leaving the farm for a visit to Iowa wouldn't bode well for his relationship with Kallie and the kids. It killed him to fail or let anyone down, whether it be Kallie and the kids or the Helping Hands board.

But judging by the silence on the other end of the line, Will Parker wasn't backing down. And he suspected if he wanted to keep his job, he'd better make the trip.

"I understand." But after he hung up the phone, the conversation continued to plague him. Something was fishy, and this information from Will was the most he'd been able to get out of the board all week.

He returned to the living room and began playing blocks with Peter and Ainsley. Stacking them high and watching them tumble, drinking in the laughing sound of the kids' delight. Trying to decide how to make all the pieces of his life fit together.

So far, an answer eluded him.

He glanced heavenward before building another tower of blocks. *What's up Your sleeve, God?*

On her knees in the flower bed along the front of the house, Kallie yanked at weeds and made room for the annuals she'd purchased in town at Bitter Creek Nursery.

She kept mulling over Grant's compliments toward her last night—and how little he actually knew about her. Apparently he thought she had things all together. He couldn't have been more wrong.

She released a sigh. Taking care of the kids didn't come easily for her. He had no idea how many nights she'd fallen into bed and cried from exhaustion and loneliness at parenting twin infants alone. Partly hoping no one would ever discover how she'd crumbled, yet also praying for someone to pick up the broken pieces and offer compassion.

Pulling her baseball cap deeper onto her head, adjusting her ponytail through the snapback opening, she reassessed the layout she'd planned for the flowers— then couldn't help but send a cursory glance to the vegetable garden nearby. She was in the most excruciating stages of gardening, or any farming really. Watering and weeding, day after day, trusting in the process with little to show in the way of success.

Sounded a lot like her life right now. Question was, could she continue what she did day after day and believe things would work out? Or was it time to switch up a few things?

Which things she'd switch up, she didn't really want to analyze too closely—because they probably included Grant and letting him have a little bit more control. In fact, right now, it was everything she could do to just work on her flower beds and give Grant time to be with the kids alone.

Why was letting go and trusting so hard for her?

She pushed the dirt around as she thought about it. She trusted Grant to take care of the kids, to be kind and gentle with them, so why did she worry when she left the house? Maybe it had to do with old habits dying hard. Or the fact that she hadn't had anyone to rely on in so long.

But why rely on others when sooner or later they let you down?

Sunday night with Grant had been so much fun—like their early days of dating. And last night's simplicity with pizza and the kids was even better. There was something deeper about it. She almost dared to think that it could be that way all the time—with Grant as a part of their family.

No doubt about it, he sure acted like he'd changed, appeared to welcome fatherhood, its responsibilities and commitment. He nearly had her convinced. But what if his intentions didn't last? No matter how good of a guy he was, he still had other commitments—his job in Iowa and his training clinics around the country, if he ever went back to them. Which she assumed he would.

It felt like he still had one foot out the door. One day, he'd have to return to Iowa, right? Then what would happen? Life would get hectic with clinics and the rescue facility. And then the farm would shift from being a stopping point on his trips to a place he was just too busy to visit.

Eventually, like Mom, he would stop coming by altogether.

She couldn't endure any more heartache like that right now, so she couldn't let him into her heart. She couldn't get her hopes up that he would stick around this time.

When she'd finished with the flower beds, she checked her watch. Time to make supper. Peeling off her gloves, she ascended the porch steps and into the house.

Grant and the kids were in the living room. Ruby met her at the door, so Kallie gave her a bit of attention. Water was boiling on the stove, and a package of spaghetti lay beside it on the counter.

Kallie smiled. Spaghetti. A simple yet satisfying comfort food. She couldn't have asked for anything better tonight. And the fact that he'd once again started supper didn't hurt. He'd been doing that every so often, and it was always a relief to walk in from a busy day to find one more task already checked off the list.

Fits of giggles and the occasional belly laugh trickled in.

"Where is Peter? I can't find him," Grant said, which was followed by more giggles. "Peekaboo!"

More laughter. Kallie turned down the gas stove's fire so the water wouldn't boil away. Then, leaning a shoulder on the doorframe separating the two rooms, she watched Grant drape a large serving blanket over Ainsley's head. They were such nice quality squares of fabric, and big, that Kallie had used them far beyond swaddling. They were good for many functions—burp cloths, cuddle blankies, for wiping up the occasional bottle spill. And apparently, also good for hide-and-seek.

"Where is Ainsley?" Grant continued, holding his palms up as he asked the question. "I can't find her."

Peter couldn't contain his laughing as he crawled quickly to Ainsley's side. Reaching up, he grabbed hold of the blanket with both chubby hands and yanked. The cloth slid off Ainsley's head, and she squealed, her smile at least one hundred watts.

"There she is! Peekaboo!" Grant clapped, then met Kallie's gaze before dropping the cloth over Peter's head and repeating the game.

Kallie fought a giggle in an attempt to blend into the background. But it didn't last long. Soon the kids realized she was there, and any games were forgotten.

She knelt to gather them in her arms as they toddled in her direction. "Hi, my darlings!" She showered each with kisses. "I've missed you all day."

Grant inched around her and into the kitchen. "I'm going to finish supper."

"Okay, thanks." Watching his shadow pass over her, she waited for him to actually acknowledge her, but beyond his meal plans, he didn't. *He isn't here for you, Kallie. Don't forget it.* "Hey," she called out to him.

"Hey," he replied from the kitchen. "How's the farm looking?"

"Pretty good." She stood and followed the kids back into the living room. Grant's laptop was open on the sofa, facing out into the room as if he'd set it down without much thought. Probably to play with the kids.

As she looked away, three words caught her attention: *back to Iowa.*

They forced her to do a double take. Her eyes zipped over the short email.

When can we set up that meeting to discuss our phone conversation? Let me know when you're back in Iowa.
—Will

"That's from one of the board members."

Kallie jumped. Grant watched her from the doorway, his expression unreadable. "I'm so sorry. I didn't mean to read your email. I just saw 'back to Iowa,' and I didn't know what it meant—"

"It's fine." He shook his head. "Yeah, Will Parker—the guy I work with on the board—he called with some new information about the rescue."

"And they need you back in Iowa?"

He shrugged, like it wasn't a big deal, but she could easily read the conflict in his eyes. "They just want to meet. I told him I couldn't, but he's pretty adamant."

"It's that important?"

He hesitated, but he finally told her what Will had said on the phone. "It's just not the right thing to do for the dogs," he said. "But this meeting is terrible timing. I don't want to go right now. Not when we've just started figuring out a new routine here."

Honestly, she didn't, either. No doubt, Grant had been great this past week. Having a couple of days to herself had been good for her mental health, and of course there were all the other ways he'd helped out. Even giving her another adult to talk to. And laugh with. He seemed to really mean it, that he didn't want to go back to Iowa right now. But she didn't want to be the cause of contention between him and his employers.

Kallie turned her gaze to Ruby, who'd taken a seat beside her, imagining all those dogs just like her, waiting to be adopted by families who loved them. "Do you think going down there will help your case?"

"Don't worry about it, Kallie." He waved it away. "I'll figure it out."

"Well, I think you should go. I don't want you losing your job on account of us."

Grant's dark green-brown eyes met hers as if he were trying to gauge her seriousness. "I know it'll do more good than teleconferencing from here," he admitted at last. "But I made a promise to you and the kids, and I intend to keep it."

The sincerity in his voice sank deeply into her skin, sparking warmth in her bones. "What if we come with you?"

His brows rose. "Come with me? To Iowa?"

"Sure, why not? June is a relatively slow month, and I could ask Mr. and Mrs. Millard to watch the place for a couple of days. It'd just be a quick trip down and back, right?"

"Well, I think so—"

"Then let's do it," she said before her nerves told her to back out of what surely was a foolish idea. "It'll be fun. I haven't left the area since Dad's last major doctor's appointment, and to be honest, I'm kind of going stir-crazy." She blushed at her admittance. "I'd love a change of scenery. And a trip that isn't medical related."

He seemed to think it through, his gaze going out of focus. Then he met hers full-on, with something like anticipation glinting there. "You think Brendan's parents will help?"

She smiled. "I can sure get them on the phone and find out."

* * *

Iowa's rolling countryside turned into city as Kallie stared out the windshield of her truck. She and Grant had taken turns driving, and now it was his turn, which was only logical since he knew how to navigate the Cedar Falls to reach Helping Hands headquarters—or at least the makeshift office space they'd created a few blocks from the burned site.

"Not long now." Grant flashed her a quick smile before turning back to the road.

Kallie smiled in return and felt another wave of butterflies filling her chest. It didn't make sense that she'd be nervous to see Grant's place of work. The only reason she could imagine was if she was afraid of him missing his job so much—or them needing him back permanently—that he wouldn't come back to the farm as he'd promised.

More and more this week, he'd given her reasons to hope he'd stick things out—for the kids' sake, of course. But hope was a fragile thing, and she knew how passionate he was about his job.

"I'm meeting the board members right when we get there," Grant began, breaking through her thoughts. "I called them when we stopped for gas so they'd know when to meet me at the office. While that meeting goes on, feel free to do whatever. Let the kids play in the lobby, go for a walk with the stroller, drive around town…whatever you'd like." He shot her a sympathetic look. "I don't know how long it'll take."

"No problem. Don't worry about us." She touched his arm but instantly regretted it. The muscle there beneath his sleeve had her heart scampering at a speed she wasn't comfortable with. "We'll manage." She slid her hand back into her own lap.

She trained her thoughts on something else as they pulled into a parking lot before a humble strip mall. Grass grew from the cracks along the concrete out front and the cracked, yellowed strip mall sign hinted at a couple of decades ago, but Grant had said this was only their temporary location—just until they could rebuild. And in that moment, Kallie was more thankful than ever that the rescue facility's current policy was to house their dogs in foster homes.

One office had a Helping Hands sign propped in the window, and Grant found an open parking space nearby. Stepping from the air-conditioned pickup truck, Kallie stopped short at the sudden blast of Iowan humidity. They quickly unloaded the kids and headed for the office door.

Serene music from a radio met them upon entering. And an empty front desk.

Grant glanced at the desk before scanning the maze of office-size rooms farther in. "Carol?"

"Back here!" A female voice carried from deeper within the building.

Must've been the secretary. Kallie followed Grant down the hall, picturing a pleasant woman in her forties with shoulder-length dark hair and kind eyes. They turned into a room and found the woman hunched over a Llewellin setter, who stood on a scale that resembled a floor mat.

But she was definitely not a brunette. Or in her forties.

The woman looked up, her curly red hair bouncing,

and Kallie quickly realized she had to be fresh out of high school or in the beginning years of college—not much younger than Grant's and her age. Sporting an athletic build, she brightened into a wide grin at the sight of Grant.

"Hey there, Sparky!" Delightful freckles splashed across her nose and cheeks, and her red ponytail bounced effortlessly as she leaped forward, slugging Grant in the arm. "Thought you got lost out there on the prairie."

Grant chuckled. "Hey, Carol. This is Kallie, and, well, my kids, Ainsley and Peter."

"Oh, yeah. Will told us about your surprise waiting on the farm." For the first time, Carol's eyes flitted to meet Kallie's, her unwavering grin still as shiny as ever. "Hey, I'm Carol."

"Hi, I'm Kallie." Kallie reached her free hand out to Carol, who gave it a quick shake before turning back to Grant.

"How was your trip back?"

"Uneventful," he said, turning his gaze upon Peter, who tentatively watched everything from his arms. "That's the way we like it, don't we? These kiddos are great travelers."

"I bet that's nice."

"Yep." Grant motioned to the dog, who'd moved off the scale in an effort to sniff around Kallie's feet. "This one's new."

"Yeah, her name is Lola, and has a brand-new litter." Carol motioned over her shoulder to a large wooden box Kallie had somehow missed when she'd walked in. "Four puppies close to being weaned. The owner couldn't take them all when she moved in with her new husband. They decided Helping Hands was the best option for Lola and her puppies."

Grant gasped at Peter. "Puppies? You wanna see 'em?"

Kallie followed him to the whelping box in the back corner, where four puppies squirmed and climbed over each other inside the wooden walls, kept warm by a couple of towels splayed out underneath them. Each was predominantly white, though black and chestnut ticking smattered their cute little energetic bodies, as their spots generally grew darker with age. One had a black splotch across one eye and cheek, which made Kallie smile as it reminded her of one of Dad's old dogs from years ago, and their newborn-puppy whimpers dug deeply into her heart.

"Oh, they're adorable," she murmured. "Look, Ainsley. Do you see the puppies?"

Grant knelt beside the box, helping Peter see better. "A puppy says, 'Woof-woof-woof.'" He gave Peter's belly a little tickle, pulling forth a giggle. Then he glanced at Carol. "Are they healthy enough to handle?"

"Yep, vet checked them out already. They're good to go. Lola is, too. All we have to do now is find a foster home for them all."

Grant had set Peter on the ground in front of his crouched figure and had gently selected a puppy from the box. Peter squealed and reached out to touch it. "Nice and gentle, bud. Nice and gentle."

Kallie watched as Grant guided Peter's hand across the puppy's back, his soft voice coaching his son how to respect animals the way he did.

Ainsley tugged on the box, reaching for the puppies and crying out in excitement.

"Shh-shh." Kallie positioned Ainsley closer to the whelping box. "Do you want to see a puppy?"

"Here, little miss." Grant scooted Peter and himself closer, cradling the puppy for Ainsley to run her fingers over.

Her hand touched the soft fur, and she giggled. "Pup-pup!" she exclaimed, then reached for it again.

Kallie laughed softly. "Yes, puppy. Isn't he sweet?"

The grins on her children's faces warmed her heart like nothing else could. Softly, she brushed an errant curl off Ainsley's forehead. The kids were growing and learning and changing right before her eyes—and she couldn't be prouder.

Her knee brushed against Grant's and she raised her gaze to meet his dark eyes. His laugh lines softened as his grin relaxed into a knowing smile. One that reached deeply into her soul, connecting her heart to his, in a way that only a mom and dad could share.

He winked and her heart rate tripled.

Somewhere in the background, she heard the front door chime. Carol piped up, something about that probably being the board members.

Grant broke eye contact with her, his brow creasing a little as he turned his focus to the door.

Purposefully this time, Kallie reached out and placed her hand on his arm. His eyes flicked to hers.

"You can do this," she whispered.

One corner of his mouth twitched upward. "Thanks." His big hand gently landed on hers before he passed off the puppy and their son, stood and left the room.

*Lord, please help him do well.*

"Grant's a good guy, isn't he?"

Kallie glanced over her shoulder at Carol, who had positioned herself on a chair, her fingers threaded in Lola's long coat. She smiled down at Kallie with her chin tilted slightly up.

"He is."

"And he has such a way with animals," Carol continued. "You should see him with all these dogs. And the way he leads this organization? Let me tell you, he has a gift."

Unease began to filter through Kallie. "Yeah, I—"

"It's too bad he'll have to hop back and forth, you know? Between here and South Dakota. He's such an asset at this facility. We don't run as well when he's gone."

Carol zeroed in on Kallie with an unwavering stare. Hmm. Well, two could play that game.

Kallie didn't blink. "Yep, too bad he's such a tremendous father who'd do anything to be there for his kids. We sure don't need any more of those in the world."

Carol dropped her smile, her eyes narrowing slightly. Then she stood, leash in hand. "He'll wind up back here. You'll see." She turned to leave. "He lives and breathes dog rescue, and we've been his family through thick and thin. Sooner or later, he'll come back to Iowa for good."

She opened the door and left.

Kallie stared at the door a few seconds longer before returning her attention to the kids, albeit distracted this time.

It pained her to think that Carol might be right. Grant cared deeply for his dogs, and it seemed that if he didn't fight for his beliefs on how they should be treated, Helping Hands was going to change their policies. Would he feel the threat and pull away from his promise at the farm?

Kallie let the kids look at the puppies for a while longer, until they seemed to lose interest. Then she walked them out of the room and back down the hall to the front desk. With Carol still in the back somewhere with Lola, the entry was unoccupied, which suited Kallie fine. She took a seat on the one chair that made up the crude waiting room, both kids on her lap.

One glance around the floor told her she wasn't confident in letting the kids down to explore—who knew what surprises they'd find?—but thankfully, she'd thought to pack a couple toys and books in the diaper bag.

She selected one of the kids' favorite touch-and-feel books and settled in to read it.

The kids listened intently, pointing at the bright colors and running their hands over the textured surfaces. She had no idea how long Grant's meeting would last, so she read slowly, taking extra care to point out every detail on each page before flipping to the next.

But surprisingly, she'd barely made it to the third page before she heard a door open, followed by a slew of footsteps and the occasional male voice.

Leading the way into the entry was Grant. Turning, he murmured, "Thank you," before giving everyone a quick handshake. A few of the men glanced at her but didn't offer any greeting.

Then Grant left the group, scooped up the diaper bag

and reached to lift Ainsley. Kallie lifted Peter and her purse and silently followed Grant outside.

The high sun warmed her arms and face as they crossed the small parking lot. She peeked at Grant, but he kept his eyes trained on the pickup ahead.

They loaded the kids, then hopped in themselves, and he started the engine.

Finally, Kallie couldn't take it anymore. "How'd it go?"

Grant put the pickup in Reverse and backed out of the parking space. "Well...we disagreed on most things. Then they let me go."

Kallie's eyes widened. "They let you go?"

"Yep." He put the truck into Drive and headed for the street.

She stared at him. He seemed to be acting nonchalant about the whole issue. "How do you feel about it?"

He shrugged.

Then understanding dawned and she turned her focus out the windshield. He was saving face. Pushing through the shock. Dealing with loss in a masculine way that was so different from how she coped with things.

She laid her hand on his shoulder and squeezed. "I'm so sorry."

He sent her a grateful look before turning back to his driving. "Thanks."

This was certainly a turn of events Kallie hadn't seen coming, especially after hearing Carol gush about Grant's irreplaceable role here. Where was God going with all of this? Out her window, Kallie watched buildings go by as the question swirled in her mind.

# Loyal Readers
# FREE BOOKS Voucher

## We're giving away THOUSANDS of FREE BOOKS

LOVE INSPIRED
INSPIRATIONAL ROMANCE

### A Hopeful Harvest
RUTH LOGAN HERNE

you can't always pick who you fall for...

LARGER PRINT

**Romance**

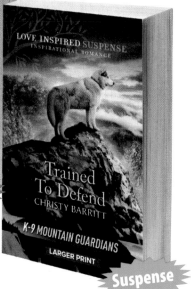

LOVE INSPIRED SUSPENSE
INSPIRATIONAL ROMANCE

### Trained To Defend
CHRISTY BARRITT

K-9 MOUNTAIN GUARDIANS

LARGER PRINT

**Suspense**

# Get up to 4 FREE FABULOUS BOOKS You Love!

To thank you for being a loyal reader we'd like to send you up to 4 FREE BOOKS, absolutely free.

Just write "YES" on the Loyal Reader Voucher and we'll send you up to 4 Free Books and Free Mystery Gifts, altogether worth over $20, as a way of saying thank you for being a loyal reader.

Try **Love Inspired® Romance Larger-Print** books and fall in love with inspirational romances that take you on an uplifting journey of faith, forgiveness and hope.

Try **Love Inspired® Suspense Larger-Print** books where courage and optimism unite in stories of faith and love in the face of danger.

Or **TRY BOTH!**

We are so glad you love the books as much as we do and can't wait to send you great new books.

So don't miss out, return your Loyal Reader Voucher Today!

*Pam Powers*

# LOYAL READER
# FREE BOOKS VOUCHER

**YES! I Love Reading, please send me up to 4 FREE BOOKS and Free Mystery Gifts from the series I select.**

Just write in "YES" on the dotted line below then return this card today and we'll send your free books & gifts asap!

➡ YES ⬅

Which do you prefer?

| ☐ **Love Inspired Romance®** Larger Print 122/322 IDL GNQS | ☐ **Love Inspired Suspense®** Larger Print 107/307 IDL GNQS | ☐ **BOTH** 122/322 & 107/307 IDL GNQ4 |

|  |  |
|---|---|
| FIRST NAME | LAST NAME |

ADDRESS

| | |
|---|---|
| APT.# | CITY |

| | |
|---|---|
| STATE/PROV. | ZIP/POSTAL CODE |

**READER SERVICE—Here's how it works:**

Accepting your 2 free books and 2 free gifts (gifts valued at approximately $10.00 retail) places you under no obligation to buy anything. You may keep the books and gifts and return the shipping statement marked "cancel." If you do not cancel, approximately one month later we'll send you 6 more books from each series you have chosen, and bill you at our low, subscribers-only discount price. Love Inspired® Romance Larger-Print books and Love Inspired® Suspense Larger-Print books consist of 6 books each month and cost just $5.99 each in the U.S. or $6.24 each in Canada. That is a savings of at least 17% off the cover price. It's quite a bargain! Shipping and handling is just 50¢ per book in the U.S. and $1.25 per book in Canada*. You may return any shipment at our expense and cancel at any time — or you may continue to receive monthly shipments at our low, subscribers-only discount price plus shipping and handling. *Terms and prices subject to change without notice. Prices do not include sales taxes which will be charged (if applicable) based on your state or country of residence. Canadian residents will be charged applicable taxes. Offer not valid in Quebec. Books received may not be as shown. All orders subject to approval. Credit or debit balances in a customer's account(s) may be offset by any other outstanding balance owed by or to the customer. Please allow 3 to 4 weeks for delivery. Offer available while quantities last.

# Chapter Six

The Great America Hotel circled the outdoor pool with all its rooms facing in. Stars dotted the darkening sky overhead as Grant leaned against the hotel wall near his room. The pool's surface shimmered green and blue, casting everything in a faint aquamarine light that ebbed and flowed.

A couple of families had set up at a picnic table on the other side of the fenced-in pool. Looked like they were celebrating a birthday party for one of their kids.

Grant's thoughts stretched into the future. He'd missed one of the twins' birthdays, yes. But Lord willing, he'd never miss another. He needed to be there, to cut the cake and help them learn to rip the wrapping paper—knowing Kallie, she'd probably taught them to open presents gently, at the tape, so as not to tear anything. Crazy gal. Who hated ripping wrapping paper anyway?

A sense of pride surged through Grant. Those kids were the best thing that had ever happened to him. Now that he'd met them, he couldn't even begin to imagine life without them.

He pulled out his phone and started typing out a new text.

The door to Kallie's hotel room opened beside him and she stepped out. He pocketed his phone. "I was just texting you."

"Funny," she said, smiling at him as she silently shut the door. "What were you going to say?"

"Just gonna see if you'd come out here after the kids were down." He noticed she'd changed out of her shorts and T-shirt into jeans and a baggy sweatshirt, as nights were still a bit chilly. And she'd gathered her long hair up into a tangled bun that still looked cute even though it was all twisted up.

"Are the kids asleep?" he asked.

"Yes, finally." She showed him the baby monitor she had tucked in her sweatshirt pouch and shook her head, her grin widening. "They're getting quite the little personalities. Tonight, they were making each other laugh. I set them up in two Pack 'N Plays, and they were giggling at each other through the mesh."

"Nice."

"Hopefully you'll get to see them do that sometime."

"Yeah, that'd be great." He would have helped with the nighttime routine tonight, but he'd been on the phone with his mom about his job situation, and then she'd shared about a struggle she was facing right now, too.

A struggle that he kept trying to push away after the call ended, but he still hadn't done so successfully. Maybe that was why he'd wound up out here by the pool, staring at another family having a good time, and wishing Kallie would join him.

She crossed her arms. "Chillier out here than I thought it'd be."

"Well, you're standing out where the breeze can catch you." He motioned with a nod. "Come closer to the wall where I am."

With a shy smile, she scooted closer. Grant fought the sudden urge to wrap his arm around her shoulders by pushing his hands deeper into his jeans pockets.

Back pressed against the door of his room, he angled a look at her face. Would she be receptive if he opened up?

"I'm sorry about your job," Kallie began before he could say anything. "I know I've told you that already, but I just feel bad that it's all because of us."

He frowned. "Because of you?"

"If you hadn't been in South Dakota this whole time, you'd probably still have your job."

"No, Kallie. It has nothing to do with you. I chose to stay at the farm. And anyway, I think they've been trying to edge me out of the job for a long time. I just never saw it until now. There's this new donor they're excited about. Lots of money. But he's got certain stipulations."

Kallie nodded her understanding. "The way he wants the rescue run."

"Yeah, that—and I found out today who it is. This guy, Charlie Erikson. He was a big-name dog trainer. But he got in trouble with the American Kennel Club a few years back for forging bloodline paperwork. Ruined his reputation and was permanently banned from the association."

"Wow. They're serious about this sort of thing, sounds like."

"Very. Anyway, he's sore about his failures. And since he was caught while teaching at a clinic with me, he's kind of had it out for me ever since. It was pure coincidence that his crimes caught up with him while we were together, but he blames me anyway. Something about trying to keep up with the up-and-coming young bucks." He shrugged. "I guess that's me."

Kallie's brows rose, her understanding deepening. "So he had you fired as part of his stipulations?"

"I can't prove it, but I think so. The pieces of the puzzle all came together for me when I found out he was their new major sponsor."

A slight breeze picked up, bringing Kallie a little closer. "Okay, but why would the board stoop to that? Bowing to some guy who's proven to be shady in the past?"

"Money makes people do weird things sometimes," Grant said. "We lost a grant earlier this year, and the building burned down, too. It's been a hard couple of quarters. Point is, I'm out now. And while I'm surprised, I know it'll be fine. I'll find something else to do, and I've still got the kids."

Nodding slightly, Kallie focused her gaze on the pool. "They're happy to have you in their lives. I think they recognize you now."

"One day, I'll get them to say 'Daddy.'"

"Yep, one day."

She stood close enough for him to wrap her in a hug. And had it been a different time and circumstance, he would have. But trust. He was still working on proving himself to her. So it was time to change the subject, to let Kallie into the thoughts that were bothering him.

"So, I just got off the phone with my mom a few minutes ago."

"How's she doing?"

"Okay." Grant glanced at the stars, exhaling and wishing he could make sense of his thoughts. "During a routine mammogram the other day, her doctor found an unusual mass."

"What?" Arm brushing against his, Kallie swiveled to look at him. "Is she okay?"

"She seems to be. Taking it better than I am."

Her hand slid around the underside of his bicep. "What's the next step?"

"She has to go in for more testing. I don't know when that'll happen, or when she'll know results."

"Wow." Kallie paused, as if thinking through the scenario. "I'm sorry. I'll be praying about her."

"Thanks." He shrugged, wishing it would deflect his stunned state, and repositioned his shoulder blades firmly against the door. "I think it's just a precaution to make sure it's not something dangerous, but the whole situation still has me thinking I need to go see her." He hadn't seen her in at least a year—had just been so busy with clinics and the facility. But what good were all those things if he missed precious time with family?

"Well, let's stop there on our way home."

His brows drew together. "You'd be okay with that?"

"Sure, it's Norfolk, Nebraska, not Timbuktu." She smiled. "And even if it were, it's your mom we're talking about. You should see her. It's totally worth the detour to get home."

The family across the pool laughed as the child ripped wrapping paper off a present and let forth an excited scream at whatever was inside. Grinning, Kallie broke their stare to peer at them. "Looks like they're having fun over there."

"Yep. I was just thinking earlier I need to teach the kids how to rip the wrapping paper off presents like that kid."

"That's right. And if you don't, I will."

"What? No, you never rip wrapping paper."

"Yes, I do."

"No, you carefully tear it off at the tape and don't even leave so much as a wrinkle."

Kallie laughed. "That's your sister, not me."

Grant raised a brow. "Jill? No way."

"Yes!"

"Okay, smarty-pants. We'll settle this when we get to Norfolk."

"You're on."

Kallie's blue eyes glittered with challenge, and Grant couldn't get over how beautiful she looked just now.

Or any time, really. She was captivating. Two years hadn't changed his attraction to her. All he wanted to do was take her in his arms. Somehow find something that made sense.

But two years had definitely changed their relationship, and it would never be what it once was. He dared to hope they could actually be friends after all this— but more than that? She probably wouldn't give him another chance.

But there was a big part of him that wanted to try anyway.

\* \* \*

Jill's house stood on a small acreage not far from town, though far enough to feel secluded. Grant had said it was a furnished rental and that the owners were on a long-term mission trip overseas. It had worked out for Jill to acquire this place and keep it up while building her business as a hairdresser until she could afford her own house in town. And Kallie guessed it was also nice to have the company of her mom, rather than living here alone without family nearby.

Grant had turned onto the gravel road that wound past the property, but then he'd promptly pulled off onto the shoulder.

Kallie looked to him. "What are we doing?"

"Taking a minute."

"Are you okay?"

"I think so." He turned to her. "Are you okay?"

"I think so?" She'd feel better if she knew what was up.

"Because they know about the kids, and they know we're not a couple—but I don't know how they'll treat us."

"You mean how they'll treat *me*." For keeping the kids a secret.

Her actions had had consequences that reached further than she'd originally imagined. When she hadn't disclosed Peter and Ainsley to Grant, she'd ultimately kept them from everyone in his family.

"I mean, I'm sure they'll be kind," he clarified, "but I don't know how awkward it'll be."

"That's okay. I get it." She tried to smile, but it came out a little on the wobbly side.

"You're sure?"

"I'm sure. Let's go."

Grant put the pickup in Drive and drove the last hundred yards to the circle drive belonging to Jill's house. He parked and got out to unbuckle Ainsley from her car seat, Kallie working on Peter's on the other side.

A boisterous bark came from the kennel in the back.

"I cannot believe you got another dog while we were there," Kallie said. "Going back this morning before we were awake. Sneaky."

Grant grinned, and only showed a hint of remorse. She would have preferred a tad more. "I've had my eye on this dog for a couple of months. I wanted to get him into a permanent home while I still could."

"I thought you were going to check on your car?" His '52 Mercedes-Benz, a classic car that he'd bought as an old junker from a hunting buddy. Now restored, it was apparently worth a pretty penny.

Grant had recognized its potential and had worked to make it all it could be. He often saw the potential in things and had to see them through until the end. Hence the two-year-old bird dog pup in Grant's truck bed right now.

A dog he hadn't considered mentioning to her until it was already adopted. She recognized it was his money, his decisions. But at the same time, the dog was coming to land that she co-owned, to interact with Ruby and the kids. She would have at least appreciated a heads-up.

"And you named him Dakota."

"Hey, after his new home."

The front door opened—almost as if they'd been watching from the window.

Nancy Young laughed as she hurried down the porch steps, her arms outstretched. "Well, this is just the grandest surprise!"

Holding Peter, Kallie hung back a few steps so that Grant went ahead of her. He stepped into his mom's arms, with Ainsley in his, and from Kallie's view, Nancy's grin couldn't have been brighter.

"I couldn't believe it when you called and said you were only a couple of hours away."

"Yeah," Grant said, "I could have told you last night when we decided to come, but I didn't figure you'd like waiting that long."

Nancy laughed some more. "You know me well, my boy. *Grandma* doesn't like to wait." She gently pushed back from Grant's hug so she could get a good look at Ainsley. "My, my. You are precious! Hello, sweet thing. You must be Ainsley Elise. I'm Grandma. I love you." It was obvious she wanted to take Ainsley in her arms, but her spirited baby wasn't quite ready to leave Grant for someone brand-new. Not yet. But Kallie had full confidence it wouldn't be long before Ainsley ventured out.

"Which makes this Peter Allen, of course." Nancy headed toward Kallie.

It was sweet that Nancy used their middle names— Grant must have told them what they were. Just extra evidence that these babies were already loved here, filling Kallie with relief.

And then Nancy did something Kallie hadn't expected. She wrapped them both in a hug without a hint of hesitation. "Glad to have you here, Kallie," she whispered in her ear.

Kallie's heart warmed. "Glad to be here," she murmured in return. "How are you doing?"

Nancy must have known Kallie referred to the medical tests, because she waved away the question. "Oh, no one wants to hear about all that. I want to meet my darling grandson."

While Nancy showered kisses and compliments over Peter, Kallie glanced up at Grant. He and Ainsley had moved to the porch, where Jill had stepped out of the house, a purse-size dog at her ankles. Their embrace spoke of their shared history and the close relationship only shared by siblings—something Kallie had never known, being an only child.

Peter leaned out of her arms, bringing her attention back. She reached to catch him but realized he was trying to get to Nancy. "Well, that's interesting. Of either baby, he isn't the one I would've guessed being the first to warm up."

"Grandma has the magic touch," Nancy cooed and laughed a low, rich, buttery laugh as Peter snuggled right in, draping his arm around her shoulder like he belonged there. "Come on. Let's go inside, shall we?" She winked at Kallie and headed for the house.

Kallie fell in line beside Nancy, carrying only the diaper bag. It was a rare moment of walking any distance without holding at least one baby in her arms. The extra help felt nice—but also a little strange.

They filed into the house, Nancy ahead of her, leading them into the living room. "Have you guys eaten? We were just about to sit down for lunch."

"No, not yet." Though Kallie's stomach was starting to growl. On the way out to Jill's, she'd been so busy thinking, brainstorming how to earn and save more money for Dad's bills that she hadn't paid any attention to the clock. If she would have, she'd have had everyone eat before arriving so as not to inconvenience their hosts by their last-minute arrival.

And to make matters worse, she hadn't come up with any other viable moneymaking ideas.

"Let me see this little guy." Jill approached her mom and tilted her head to catch Peter's attention. "Hey, there, mister. You're right, Grant. He looks just like you—except he's cute."

"Hey!" Grant's voice carried back from the kitchen.

Laughing, Jill made eye contact with Kallie, and both froze for a millisecond. What was Jill thinking? The protective nature behind Grant's sister's eyes was starkly clear, and suddenly the mountain Kallie needed to climb to atone for her sins seemed infinitely taller.

"Hey, Jill." Better to make the first, friendly move. "I love your home. And thanks for letting us visit on such short notice."

Jill slowly smiled. "Thanks. And also, thanks for bringing the kids by." She turned back to Peter. "It's fun to meet my niece and nephew."

By this time, they'd trickled into the kitchen, Nancy chatting a mile a minute. "We were just about to make sandwiches," she was saying. "But I took the liberty of making something I thought the kids might like. Hope that's okay. What do they think of peas?"

"Love them." Grant eased himself into one of the blond wooden chairs at the traditional-style table. "The more the better."

"I also have shredded chicken and cooked carrots. They'd like those, right?"

"Perfect, Mom. Hey, Jill. Who is this little mop that keeps nipping at my shoelaces?"

Jill's hands popped onto her hips. "That's Pepper, and she's a cockapoo. Also, she's an excellent judge of character."

Kallie hid a grin as she placed the diaper bag out of the way on the counter. Heavy thing. She needed to clean it out sometime. She didn't know anyone who packed as much as she did.

"I'm just kidding. Trying to press my sister's buttons, that's all."

"Right back at you, bro."

Peeking over her shoulder, Kallie watched him reach down and pet Pepper's curly golden hair, using the same affection he used when greeting Bella, Chief and Ruby. On his lap, Ainsley made a few eager noises, reaching for Pepper, and Grant spoke quietly to her about the puppy.

In search of Peter, she looked over her other shoulder. He still clung to Nancy, and she was telling him about yummy peas and carrots as Jill blew on a warm spoonful before giving him a taste.

Both kids were taken care of. Not much for Kallie to do but wander over to the opened loaf of bread and deli meat to make herself a sandwich. She should relax into this unexpected moment of free time. Breathe easy, knowing these kids were loved and watched after. So why did she suddenly feel unneeded? And even more so, invisible?

* * *

"Okay, Mom. When do you get the next test done? You said you were going to call down to the clinic today and see."

Bobbing Peter on his knee and wrangling Dakota with a tug-of-war chew toy, Grant had taken up residence on the floral couch. In a chair opposite the couch, Ainsley sat on Mom's lap, while Jill was in the kitchen preparing popcorn and snacks that she'd insisted were necessary staples, regardless of what activity was taking place. So long as the family was involved, it was a celebration-type night.

Kallie sat beside him, hands sandwiched between her legs, looking about as relaxed as a cactus.

"I go in for my test on Monday."

So a few more days to pray, as today was Friday. "And when will we get test results?"

"Should be the same day. As of yet, I won't be having a biopsy done or anything." Mom stared at him pointedly. "Son, there's nothing to worry about. I shouldn't have told you."

"Do you have insurance to cover all this?"

"Yes."

"Because if you do need extensive testing, or it turns out to be cancer, you're going to need that protection."

"You worry too much."

"You're my mom. You worried about us for eighteen years. It's time for me to return the favor."

At that, Mom smiled. "Honey, have faith that everything will work out. Cancer or no cancer. God's in control, and He takes care of His children. That's a promise."

Kallie's hand suddenly slipped onto his knee, touch as light as the volume of her voice. "We should probably get the kids to bed."

Grant glanced at the clock, then peered around Peter to see his face. Perfectly timed, the little rock star yawned and rubbed his eyes.

"Sounds good." He stood, and Kallie retrieved Ainsley before they headed down the hall to what would be Kallie's and the kids' room for the night. Dakota trailed them the entire way and even slipped inside. Thankfully, in Kallie's room, the pup rolled up with his chew toy and entertained himself while the kids went to sleep.

It took Grant and Kallie a while to get Peter and Ainsley to settle down—Grant chalked it up to being in a new location and having too much sleep during the day while traveling. Partway through, he got a text from Jill saying that Mom had gone to bed and she had headed out to do hair for a friend's wedding—quick to joke that maybe she could have moved it if she'd had any heads up that Grant was going to be in town.

He still smiled at that last part as he followed Kallie and Dakota out into the hallway and quietly shut the bedroom door on the sleeping babies. Jill would joke with Grant until the cows came home, but it took her a long time to become that comfortable with someone. Honestly, he didn't think she'd opened up that much with anyone else since Alec, her high school boyfriend who'd passed away just after graduation. She'd sort of shut down after that. Moved to Nebraska, got her hairdresser license. It was good to see her joking around now.

He slipped into the kitchen, Kallie following him. "Good thing Jill made all this food and then left so we could eat it all," he said.

"I'm feeling up to the challenge tonight." Kallie grabbed a big plastic cup from a stack on the counter before scooping it deep into the ginormous bowl of popcorn. "What about you?"

He couldn't be shown up. That was for sure. "Oh, you can count on it."

They loaded up on snacks and decided on a whim to head out the back door. After finding a soft spot on the grass just beyond the patio, they settled in with Dakota next to them, a spray of stars overtaking the darkening sky. Donned in sweatshirts, they didn't have to worry much about the nuisance of mosquitoes. Even if they had, Grant doubted he would notice with Kallie sitting beside him. He began to relax, to enjoy the near-stillness of this place, rather than feeling stir-crazy by the quiet like he used to.

Though this may not be the relaxing evening he'd thought it would be—judging by the way Kallie released a long breath as if she'd been holding it on her shoulders for a while now.

He angled a look at her from beneath his ball cap. "You've been awfully quiet today. Everything okay?"

Kallie stared out over the prairie. She seemed to consider his question, then shrugged. "Just tired, I guess."

No way. She wasn't fooling him. Kallie was usually quiet, but something was off this time. "Are you concerned about the Millards watching the farm?"

"What? No."

"Something up with the kids?"

"No."

Grant waited. She didn't move, didn't offer any more explanation. He pressed his lips together. "Kallie. Don't go silent on me again like you used to. You know I can't read your mind."

"Maybe I don't want you to."

Okay. Obviously something was going on. And he intended to get to the bottom of it.

"Does it have something to do with being here? At Jill's and Mom's?"

"Grant, I—no, it's good we're here. Really. They needed to see the kids, and you needed to see your mom."

"But?"

"Stop digging for it, please. I don't want to talk about it."

Her voice shook a little, which meant he'd hit a nerve. Darkness of evening crept over them. He lifted his hand and placed it on her shoulder, the warmth there beneath his hand tempting him to move his fingers up to the nape of her neck, to massage the muscles there like he used to. But now he had no right. And obviously, he had a lot more work to do before she'd trust him enough to let him in.

Common sense told him to back down and talk about something else. But he never was much good at common sense.

"Kal, I know it's hard being here. For a long time, it's just been you, Frank and the kids. And now there are more and more people coming into their lives. I don't blame you for struggling to adjust to the change."

Her brows rose. "Struggling to adjust?"

"Yeah, I—"

"Well, pardon me for deciding to raise my kids the way I thought was best, and then had my plans pulled out from under me."

"Are you regretting telling me about the kids?"

"I'm still deciding." She dropped her gaze to the grass in front of her, and Grant removed his hand from her shoulder.

"Wow." Taking the blow of her words like a punch to the chest, he pulled off his hat and scratched at his hair. That wasn't exactly the answer he was expecting.

"I just…" Faltering, Kallie shook her head. "Never mind."

He flicked his stare to her profile. Even in the darkness, he could read her taut expression, the myriad of thoughts colliding in her mind. He slipped the ball cap back on his head with renewed determination.

"You know what, Kallie? I don't believe you. I don't think you're regretting anything. I think you're just scared."

Kallie shot him a glare. "Excuse me?"

"You heard me loud and clear, darlin'. I think you like being a part of a community and that scares you because you're so used to doing everything on your own."

Blue eyes narrowed. "You think I pride myself on doing everything on my own? Then you don't know me at all."

"I'm trying my best here. You've gotta throw me a bone."

"You wanna know what it's like on my own? Okay, I'll tell you. Sometimes I've endured all day, just begging for an early bedtime for the kids, then cried myself to sleep afterward, only to be woken up a few hours later by more diaper changes and feedings and baby indigestion. More often than not, I have laundry piled up as high as the washer, and my crawl space is so full of diaper boxes, you can't even step inside. Most days, I'm so lonely, I can't think straight." Tears spilled from her eyes, and she didn't even bother wiping them away. "I feel so guilty saying that out loud. My kids are everything to me. I'd never wish them away, never long for a different life. But some days, I just…" Her words caught. Gulping, she looked away.

Loneliness. The truth of her statement hollowed him out. All he could think to do was break the barrier. He wrapped his arms around her and tucked her head into the crook of his shoulder. Placed his head on her shoulder and prayed for guidance. It didn't matter what it took—from now on, he'd find a way to make sure she wasn't lonely again.

# Chapter Seven

❧

"So, I was thinking. I might've solved our financial problem."

It was Monday afternoon, and Kallie looked up from the vegetable garden, her hands poised around a stand of weeds that had rampantly grown over the weekend. Crazy how weeds seemed to know when you were out of town.

Peter and Ainsley were exploring the yard in front of her, each with their own baby-size hats to shield their skin from the sun. Grant stood beside them, his fierce green-brown eyes showing their wild side. Yep, he'd definitely discovered some sort of project he wanted to implement. When they were dating, she'd found his big ideas romantic. Now, with so much at stake, she wasn't sure she wanted to take the risk.

With his new venture or with his heart. After Friday night in Jill's backyard, she'd decided she had disclosed too much to Grant. Sinking into his embrace had felt wonderful—achingly so—but she couldn't have him thinking she was asking for comfort. Because a close embrace wasn't going to change all that stood between them. He'd left her and she'd hidden the kids. They obviously had an issue with trust. What kind of relationship could be built on a rocky foundation like that?

"What is it?" she asked.

"I want to open my own dog training facility here."

Kallie stared at him, fairly certain that if her eyebrows shot any higher, they'd disappear beneath the brim of her ball cap. "You what?"

"Come on. It'd be fun. And extra income to boot."

"I thought you said I shouldn't get a second job."

"I did. This would mostly be me. You could help wherever you wanted to, but I'd take on the bulk of the work."

"I don't know…"

"This is something I'm serious about. I don't have another job right now, so we could use the income. You've seen the numbers firsthand and know they would help pay off loans."

She was pretty sure her internal debate read across her face like Sunday's newspaper. She was satisfied with just having Ruby to care for. Could she be okay with having all of those dogs on the property again, the business reminding her of Dad all the time?

Then again, Grant was right—they needed the money if they hoped to save the farm. The wheat wouldn't be ready for another month, and they had bills due before then. If he could pull together some clients and do a one-or two-week training, then that might float them through the rest of the month and into the next.

"It's my way of contributing—to my half, if that distinction helps you accept it. It would give me peace of mind to know I'd provided for my kids."

She sighed. "You know, I guess it's probably fine."

He stood a little straighter. "Really? You don't mind?"

"It was a lot of work when we had a training program before, and with the twins and my recent stress, I'll be honest that I'm leery of adding more to my plate." She eyed him warily. "But I know it'd be an asset to our business." And he'd enjoy it, too. Give him a chance to work with some bird dogs.

A half smile climbed his mouth, doing funky things to Kallie's heart rate. "Okay. Let's do it," he said. "I'll make some phone calls."

"Okay." Hopefully it went well—both for the farm's sake and for Grant's. "How'd your mom's test go? Has she called you?"

"Not yet." The barest flicker of worry crossed his gaze, but he hid it well. Too bad for him, Kallie knew how to read him. And she knew what it was like to wait for test results for a parent.

"I'll keep praying for her."

Grant smiled faintly. "Thanks."

"Let me know when you get the results."

"Okay, will do."

"Oh, also, I wanted to run something by you," Kallie said, sitting back on her heels. "The wheat crop is looking really good right now. Like, *really* good. Haven't seen it like this in a while."

"Great."

"So, I think we need to get hail insurance for it." She hesitated. "It's really expensive, so most people don't get it unless they need to—but I think in this case, we need to. If we were to lose this whole crop to a storm and didn't have insurance, it would be absolutely devastating."

"Got it. Call the right people. We'll make sure the money's there."

"Cool." That was a weight off her shoulders. She would do all she could to make sure this place stayed in the black. She yawned. "Sorry. We were up a lot last night. I think Ainsley's getting a tooth."

As if to emphasize that fact, Ainsley paused in her yard exploration at Grant's feet. She rubbed her eye before sticking a finger between her gums.

Smiling, Grant reached down to pick Ainsley up. Then he scooped up Peter, who wasn't far away, and cuddled both kids against his simple gray T-shirt, warming her insides more than she cared to acknowledge.

"I've got 'em," he said. "Go take a nap or something."

"What? Oh, no, I couldn't—"

"Seriously, it's fine. Let me hang out with them for a few hours. We'll drive around in the truck and go for a stroller ride. Maybe bring the dogs and let them run. It'll be fun." He shot her a knowing look. "Seriously. When do you ever get a chance to take a nap?"

She lowered her gaze. "Never."

"Exactly. Now go. The weeds will wait."

With a resigned sigh, Kallie climbed to her feet and pulled off her gloves as she headed for the garden gate. She ambled to her front door and finally slipped inside, after a long look at Grant in the yard, holding close and tickling her kids—*their* kids.

Best not to let her mind go there—though it was sure getting harder with each passing day.

They were just good friends these days. Besides, he was here on the farm for the kids, not for her. So regardless of whatever feelings might grow inside her, she still needed to make the conscious effort to keep Grant at an emotional distance. Better to never love again than to fall and be crushed a second time.

She headed through her house, eerily silent, to the stairs. In her bedroom, she lay on her bed and fell asleep not too long after her head hit her pillow.

When she awoke two hours later, she blinked, staring at the ceiling. What had awakened her? Still groggy, she sat up. Then she heard it again. A knock on the door.

Strange. Grant never knocked anymore. What was this about?

She slipped downstairs, trying to reach through her mental fog to figure out what day it was. It wasn't the day the frozen-food delivery truck stopped by. She hadn't ordered any packages online. Was Rachel here to see her? Seemed weird she hadn't called first. She usually did, just to make sure Kallie wasn't too preoccupied with the kids. Besides, she usually worked Monday afternoons.

She reached the door, glancing back at the clock on the stove. Five o'clock. Maybe it was indeed Grant and the kids. They'd be protesting for supper right about now. Tacos was a fast meal. She could have that done lickety-split.

Kallie opened the door and halted.

"Hi, hun." Mom stared back at her, the late sun lighting her slender frame and shoulder-length blond hair. Her eyes had deeper lines etched around them than last time Kallie had seen her, but her eyes themselves were the same. Albeit hesitant. "Can I come in?"

* * *

Seemed everyone already had plans for the summer.

Grant hung up his phone and placed it on his kitchen table. So much for his contacts. He'd called almost everyone he knew with a bird dog and none were available to bring their dogs out to the farm for a refresher course. Obedience, hunting; one week, two week; you name it. No one could make a training session of any kind. He still had a couple more people on his list, so he'd call them, too—though now he certainly had his doubts.

Maybe this had been a foolish idea, starting up a training center. Or at least getting one ready in time for this summer.

But it was the first time Kallie had called it "our business." That had him beaming from the inside out, and it was enough motivation for him to try anything to make it work. Doubts or no doubts, once he finished calling all of his warm leads, he'd move on to cold leads. Seriously, he'd been in charge of a nonprofit. He was used to making cold calls anyway and wouldn't stop until at least one training session was full.

And he wouldn't be like his dad, allowing every responsibility to fall to Peter and Ainsley's mom. He'd make this business work. Success meant being prepared and responsible, and if nothing else happened in his life, he'd make sure to leave that legacy for his kids.

With suppertime around the corner, Grant pushed the stroller up to Kallie's door and then unstrapped Peter. The boy cooed, pointing at the door as if he recognized it. Grant smiled. "Yep. We're home, bud."

Not that he had much experience with kids—but he was pretty sure both kiddos were sharp as whips.

Gingerly, he opened the door with Peter in his arms and found the kitchen empty. Which made him nod. Good—that meant Kallie was still sleeping. She'd seemed to need it.

"There you go." He placed Peter on the floor, who toddled a few steps before dropping to his knees so he could easily cruise into the living room, straight for his stuffed giraffe. After watching him a few seconds, Grant pivoted back to unstrap Ainsley from the stroller.

"Well, hello there, handsome!" a female voice said from the living room. "What a big boy you are."

Grant whirled around. That wasn't Kallie's voice.

Hugging Ainsley close, he rushed to the living room, only thinking of keeping Peter safe from whoever had trespassed. But the woman sitting on the recliner held a striking resemblance to Kallie, plus about twenty-five years.

"Edith?" Grant frowned. "What are you doing here?"

Edith Shore met his gaze and confusion overtook her features. She stood slowly. "Aren't you—"

"Grant Young, ma'am." Not sure what else to do, he stuck his hand out to shake hers.

"You were going to marry—"

"Yep." So glad she remembered that part. He hadn't really met her but once. When Grant started coming around the farm, Edith and Frank were only months from their divorce. He scooped Peter off the floor and held both kids close to his chest. "Where's Kallie?"

"I—I don't know. She—"

"Does she know you're here?" One thing was certain, she wouldn't be sleeping if she knew her mom was downstairs.

"Yes. I got here about ten minutes ago, and I'm afraid it upset her. She left on the four-wheeler." Edith released a shaky sigh.

The four-wheeler? "Where'd she go?"

"I don't know. Maybe I should just leave. I'd hoped to make amends, but it might be too late for that."

Her fingers fumbled together, and she looked away. Every bit her daughter's mother in mannerisms. It made Grant think of his own mom and again wish that Kallie's relationship with Edith could be restored. Sounded like Edith wanted that, too.

But first, he had to locate Kallie. Out the window, he turned his gaze up the road, long-dormant memories pushing through him. "Hmm. No, stick around. Would you mind watching the kids for a bit?"

Edith's face lit, but her smile was a bit timid. "Sure, I'd love to. If you think she wouldn't mind."

"Thanks." After making sure the kids were settled in, Grant grabbed the farm truck's keys off the nail by the screen door and made his way down the porch steps.

He had to make sure Kallie was okay. And he had a pretty good guess of where she was.

Country music pulsed over the truck's radio as he drove down the gravel road. The sun would soon be gone. *God, please let my instincts be correct.*

As his truck rumbled into a field and over the uneven path worn down by tire tracks, he scanned the area for any sign of Kallie and the four-wheeler. Slowly, he approached the empty creek bed. Cottonwoods stretched across the land, nestled in where the creek bed curved wide around a bend.

*There.*

Sure enough, Kallie sat on a fallen log beneath one such cottonwood, her four-wheeler parked not too far away. Grant stopped the truck next to it, left it running and walked the rest of the way.

The sunset painted her profile in orange and gold, like wheat during the harvest. She looked up as he approached and brushed back tears.

"What are you doing here?" she asked. "Where are the kids?"

He dug his hands into his pockets. "With your mom."

"Grant—"

"They'll be fine for a while." He took a seat beside her, propping his elbows on his knees. Then he waited, listening to the crickets and the wind rustling through the trees overhead.

Hugging her arms, Kallie turned her attention back to the empty creek bed. "It shouldn't have to be like this," she muttered. "A mom's supposed to be there for her kids. Why wasn't mine?"

Grant thought about it, then shook his head. "I don't know. Maybe she was trying to be there for you in another way."

"It's not what I needed. I didn't care if her job allowed us to get new school clothes every year, or whatever her reasoning was. I needed her here—to lean on and learn from."

"Yeah, I get it."

She swiped at another tear. "I felt like I wasn't enough, you know? Like she had to go on the road in order to find whatever it was she needed out of life."

Was that why Kallie never wanted to leave the kids'

side? Did she think she was failing as a mom if she ever had a hint of interest in something other than the kids?

Shaking his head, Grant took her hand. "You're enough, Kallie Shore. Whether anyone else ever recognizes it, you're enough."

He laced his fingers with hers. New tears welled in her eyes before she blinked and they dropped down her cheeks. With her free hand, she covered her eyes and gave a shuddered sigh.

When she let her hand fall into her lap, her gaze reached back in time, seeming to find the memories among the cottonwoods. "When I was nine, my mom left on an especially long business trip. I remember I finally got up the courage to call her and ask if she'd tuck me in when she got home. It was something she hadn't done in a while, and I'd been missing it."

Her hand tightened around his, so he scooted closer.

"She'd said of course she would, and I got so excited. I made everything extra special." Blinking a few times, Kallie shook her head. "I cleaned my room and lined up all my stuffed animals. I'd made this little sign with paper and markers that said, 'Welcome home, Mom,' and it was propped up by the animals as if they were helping me greet her when she arrived. Anyway, I wore my favorite pajamas and braided my hair and made a card I was going to give her. I had this whole speech prepared about how I'd missed her and hoped she'd never have to leave again."

A tear slipped down her cheek. Grant switched her hand into his far one so he could tug her against his side.

"So when she got home—did she tuck you in?"

She huffed. "She didn't even come home."

His hand lightly ran along her outside arm. Slowly,

she rested her head in the pocket of his shoulder and collarbone. "She'd passed right on by to the next job. Then she called the next morning to say she'd been running late and to apologize. Promised to tuck me in the next time she came home, but it didn't matter by then. I already knew I couldn't trust her with things that were important to me." Her distant stare hardened. "No one cares half as much about your wishes and dreams as you do. It's a fact of life. So why it bothers me that Mom's around all of a sudden—I don't know." As her gaze connected with Grant, she squeezed his hand further. "I shouldn't care if I've written her off, right?"

He smiled. "Maybe you haven't."

Kallie was quiet—maybe she had to think about that one. Gently, he tugged her closer to him, wishing he could help her see the worth she carried. What he saw in her.

"Look, I know what it's like to live with a parent who has squandered his life. And if I hadn't before, I also understand now how important my mom is to me. I think if I had the chance to fix my relationship with my dad the way you might with your mom, I'd jump at it. That's all I'm saying."

Seemed as if she'd relaxed into him some, though he wasn't one hundred percent sure. "You're a good friend," she finally murmured.

A good friend. Obviously, that's what she wanted him to be, and nothing more. Why couldn't he keep his heart in check, stay in the friend zone and accept it?

"Kal, there's something I've been wondering. Did your dad ever pressure you to find me and tell me about the kids?"

She took a few seconds to answer. "Yeah. And I should have. I know saying sorry will never be enough."

"Just seems odd that I'd still be in the will after we ended things."

"In the end, I was so busy with Dad that I never thought to look at the beneficiaries on the will. All I could think about was being thankful we'd already set his will up, you know? And then I spent the rest of my energy managing the farm, the kids and caring for him."

Frustration scratched through him. Why hadn't Frank contacted him? He could've helped on the place, at least for a while. Or paid for worthwhile help. Something. As it was, Grant hadn't even known Frank was sick.

She shifted her head, still on his shoulder, and tilted it slightly upward as she spoke. "Honestly though, I think he left you in on purpose."

"Yeah?"

"Yeah. He knew the kids would need you."

"Well, I need *them*. I had no idea how much until I met them."

It did hurt that he might never have known about the kids if it hadn't been for the will. But the fact was, he couldn't change the past. And he couldn't control Kallie's life decisions. The best he could do was prove himself a worthy dad—to help anywhere he could and to make her feel proud that he'd entered the kids' lives, not ashamed.

His eyes met hers and drank her in before visually outlining the curves of her face. Slowly, he let go of her hand and moved his thumb along her cheek beside her mouth. This precious woman. What had he been thinking, letting her go?

The song on the truck radio ended and another

began. Faintly, in the background, but Grant closed his eyes as the haunting tune reached into his soul and reminded him. Reminded him of the past, of the times he and Kallie had fallen in love to those very words, those very notes, two years ago.

"Do you recognize—"

"Yes." Kallie straightened off his chest. She began to move away, but he gently caught her hand. She paused, but he could feel her shoulders stiffen beneath his arm, could almost hear her breath catch as the singer crooned the words so deeply ingrained in both of them.

"Remember when we first heard it?"

After a second, she nodded. "Down here. By the empty creek bed."

"We drove down here to watch the sun set and then it came on the radio." He dared to rub his thumb against the curve of her shoulder, his chest tightening. "You said it reminded you of us."

She didn't look at him, but he knew the memories sailed through her mind.

*God, let her hear me.*

"The second time we heard it, we were in the barn, unloading a shipment of dog food," he said, his voice growing low. "And the next time was on our way home from Fourth of July fireworks, and you were so pretty in the moonlight—"

"Grant, please." Her hushed voice broke. She pressed her fingers to her eyes. "It's getting late. I've got to feed the kids and get them down for the night."

Releasing his hand, she hopped off the log.

He sat for a moment before gritting his jaw and getting up himself. He followed her to her four-wheeler, watched her fish out the key and climb aboard. She fumbled putting the key in the ignition, mumbling something unintelligible beneath her breath.

When she got the four-wheeler going, she sent him a quiet smile. "Thanks for talking me through things about my mom. It helped."

Somehow he managed to return her smile. "You're welcome. Hope it works out." His bit back anything else as he watched her drive away.

When Kallie returned to the house, Grant wasn't far behind her.

Part of her wanted to run from the feelings brewing inside her. But another part wanted his strength. Her mother was inside the house, and soon she'd be facing her and their entire past. Somehow, being around Grant made her feel more confident that she could handle it.

Kallie met Grant on the pickup's driver side, shielded from the house. "Do you want to stay for supper?" she asked.

Grant stuck his hands deep into his pockets. "I think I'd better eat on my own tonight."

Kallie frowned.

"I'd love to, honestly," he added. "But you've got some catching up to do with your mom, and I'd only be in the way."

"You wouldn't be in the way." But even as Kallie said it, she knew he was right. She needed to at least finally hear her out. And that was something they should do alone.

"Okay." She half turned, then pivoted back. "See you tomorrow."

"Yep." That slow, tantalizing grin of his slid back

into place, and she had to hurry away before he saw his smile returned.

Kallie shook her head, shoe treads scraping over the gravel turnaround. These days, her rebel grin apparently wasn't going to be contained when it came to Grant Young.

He'd surprised her. She hadn't expected him to stick around as long as he had, working the farm and getting to know the kids. It was a nice change. Hopefully it stuck.

She stepped inside and found Peter and Ainsley sitting in their high chairs. Mom was seated beside them at the table, spoon-feeding them a bowl of oatmeal—the spoon acting as an airplane coming in for a landing, and the kids were giggling at the thrilling game.

"Hey," she offered, before turning into the laundry room to scoop food out for Ruby.

"Hi, hun." Mom's voice was so familiar, it hurt. But also so foreign. How often had Kallie prayed to hear that voice in this house on a regular basis?

*Listen to what she has to say. Be open to restoring the only parent relationship you have left.*

She fed Ruby, then returned to the kitchen. Mom looked up from the kids and Kallie forced herself to sit down at the table with her.

"I wasn't sure what the kids ate these days," Mom said. "But I figured oatmeal was pretty safe."

"Oatmeal's fine."

Silence poured in. So thick she felt she'd drown.

Finally, Kallie took a breath and asked the question that had been weighing her down for the past hour. "What brings you out here?"

"I've changed a lot over the past few years, and I needed to come back and say I'm sorry."

Ainsley protested having to wait for food, so Mom paused to give her a granddaughter a bite. All the while, Kallie's mind spun with questions.

"I started going to church," Mom said.

Kallie raised her brows. That was something Mom had never done, even when home with her and Dad. "Really?"

Mom nodded. "Three months ago, I became a Christian. And—and I deeply regret missing all those formative years of your life. I want to make things right."

How was Kallie supposed to respond to that? She wanted things to be made right between them, too—but how did someone heal years of hurt?

The bowl of oatmeal went fast, and the children protested, wanting more. Kallie quickly realized this was a conversation they'd be better off having after the kids went to bed.

Turning the topic to Peter and Ainsley, they finished feeding the kids, and then after playing with them and getting them in bed, Kallie and her mom grabbed fresh coffee and moved out to the porch. The sun had completely set now, and twilight had taken over the sky in dusky blue elegance. They sat side by side, listening to the crickets' serenade. Hopefully it would make their conversation easier.

"So, who is Grant?" Mom asked, both hands around the mug on her lap. "Is he the kids' dad?"

"Yes."

Mom took a long pause before speaking again. "Where's he living these days?"

"Here, actually. In the hired help cottage. Before this, he was in Iowa, running a setter rescue facility and also putting on training clinics around the country. But once he found out about the kids, he settled here and wouldn't leave. When Grant sets his mind on something, you'll have a hard time tearing him away."

Sounded like someone else she knew—herself.

Kallie exhaled at the memory of him digging his heels in, how aggravating it had felt and how that aggravation had now turned to hope mixed with concern. "I just hope he keeps his mind focused on the kids."

"Do you think he won't?"

It took Kallie a moment to answer. "I don't know what to think yet. Jury's still out. But if Peter and Ainsley are going to have a father in their lives, it had better be a dependable one."

"Yes… You said he didn't know about the kids?"

"It's a long story." She tried telling it as succinctly as she could. "It's my fault. I have no good excuse. I was selfish and hurt. And extremely stubborn. I shouldn't have kept them a secret from him."

"Well, don't be too hard on yourself," Mom murmured, her gaze on a flock of birds swirling around the shrub oaks in the distance. "Sometimes you can't trust people. But then other people you can. It takes time to know the difference."

More aching silence broke up the conversation. So many questions, but which should she ask first? Which were even worth asking, and which were better off lost in the pages of the past?

"Are you and—"

"Why didn't—"

They gave each other awkward smiles.

"You go first," Kallie said.

"Are you and Grant back together now?"

The words swirled through Kallie's mind and she shook her head. "Oh, no. We're too different. We could never be together like that."

Mom nodded, as if she was satisfied with the brief explanation. "Okay, your turn," she said.

"Why didn't you come to Dad's funeral?"

Mom's face shadowed over with grief. "I wanted to. I really did. I'm so sorry I wasn't there. I was caregiving for my aunt Opal, who wound up passing away just last week. That's when I called you—on Sunday."

When Kallie and Grant were on their way to church together.

"There was no one else to take care of her. I didn't figure your dad or you wanted me there anyway." She sighed. "Regardless, the truth is, I missed your dad's funeral, and I've deeply regretted it. I've regretted a lot of things in my life. Especially how I left you and your dad so much."

"Why did you leave us so often? You're my mother. I needed you."

Tears filled Mom's eyes. She tried to smile but it came out wavering, so she patted Kallie's hand instead. "The whys don't matter much anymore. What matters is that I right my wrongs and make the most of the time we have left together."

Kallie lowered her eyes, wishing she'd been brave enough to answer the phone last week when Mom had called. Brave enough to do a lot of things in this life. Maybe this would be the start of a bold new beginning.

# Chapter Eight

One more sunken screw and the dog shelter would be complete. Late-afternoon sun beat down on Grant's shoulders and neck as he finished the work and climbed down his ladder. He'd spent the morning mowing a portion of grass behind the old kennels, planning to use that area for some bird and obedience training. The fields beyond were ideal for firsthand experience, catching the scent of wild birds and allowing the dogs a chance to do what they were born to do. The opportunity thrummed through his veins.

This afternoon, he'd reconstructed and secured the shelter Frank had used to keep dogs shaded and watered while awaiting their turn to train. It was in fairly good condition—only needed a few sections repaired. Which was a good thing, as their first set of bird dogs were coming in a matter of days.

Grant couldn't thank God enough for the lead he'd received during his last phone call yesterday evening. He'd spent Tuesday, Wednesday and Thursday calling people about training their dogs.

Many were interested—next summer. Helpful in the long run, but not exactly for this year. He had to save the farm first before he could think about next summer's plans.

But the last handler he'd called said he might be able to help. He personally couldn't bring his dog up from Texas, but he had a friend who might be interested in bringing his own two—said they'd heard of Grant and respected the training methods he taught at his seminars. And if his friend came, he'd send his dog with him.

Turned out, it worked perfectly for the handler's friend to deliver all three dogs for an introductory level, four-week training. Starting next Friday, a week from today. Thanks to Frank, a lot of the supplies Grant would need were already on the premises. But there were still a lot of repairs to make and schedules to design.

The best news of all was that both men had already paid their deposits. That money was about to take a nice chunk out of Frank's outstanding loans.

"Things are looking up, Chief." Grant shook his fingers through Chief's shaggy black-and-white ears. "This might be just the break we were looking for."

And as an added cherry on top of his already amazing sundae—Mom's test results had come back normal.

He'd praised God multiple times for that over the past week. It had also prompted him to think a lot about family. More than just about anything, he wanted his kids to grow up proud of their dad, not ashamed of him like Grant had been. Having his own business in a field he loved, now that was the dream. He could not only provide for his kids, but one day when he was gone, they'd inherit it. It was yet another way he could protect them long into the future. A way for him to be dependable, loyal and steadfast. Productive and successful while still being there for his kids.

As he headed for the house, he took a longer look at Chief's shaggy hair—the wavy strands hanging from his ears, the thick feathering on his chest and legs, and the long flag of his tail. He had to brush Chief quite a bit to remove all the burrs he picked up in the field. It was definitely time for a significant trim.

Frank—well, really Kallie—used to do this with all the dogs that came to camp, in order to keep them clean and as burr-free as possible during their stay. Grant seriously considered keeping up the tradition.

Leaving Chief out front to sniff around, Grant headed inside Kallie's house.

Laughing met him just inside. It died away, and Kallie and Edith looked at him from the kitchen, where—speaking of hair—they were in the middle of cutting Ainsley's and Peter's in their high chairs.

"Hey," Kallie said, her eyes bright. "They're getting haircuts for the first time. And they're *not* sure what to think of it."

The smell of supper already wafted from inside the oven, which was a pretty standard occurrence now that Edith had been here for a week, but Grant suddenly didn't feel like eating.

Peter, recognizing Grant, reached out toward him. "Ehh-ehh-ehh!"

It was nice that someone cared to include him. "Hey, bud." He thought about going over to give the boy's hand an affectionate shake, like he usually did, but as

Peter had moved, Kallie quietly shushed him and moved him back into position, murmuring something about him needing to stay still for the cut. So Grant hung back.

"Supper's almost ready," Edith said, scissors in hand. "Are you staying tonight?"

Her glance in his direction was very brief before she turned back to Ainsley's hair. But there was something in her face that he didn't quite like.

Before Edith had arrived, Grant watched the kids three times a week. This week, it'd only been for one afternoon. And Edith had been there, too, making meals and rocking the kids to sleep, sort of giving Grant the feeling of being in the way. Every other day, Edith had watched them either on her own or with Kallie.

He told himself he was overreacting. The woman had never met her grandkids and was just now reconnecting with her daughter. She needed time to do that. But that didn't make it any less frustrating, and it didn't change the fact that he felt a little put off by the way she seemed to edge him out and then fill his shoes.

"Supper?" Kallie prompted.

"No," he heard himself say, probably more out of knee-jerk reaction than anything. "I'm not hungry. Just stopped to see if you could trim Chief and Bella for me before training camp starts. Maybe trim the other dogs, too, when they come."

"Sure. I can do that."

"Great." Grant headed for the door. "See you around."

A few strides across the turnaround and he heard the door open.

"Grant?" Kallie followed him. "Are you okay?"

Her long blond hair hung around her shoulders in super-pretty waves, like maybe she'd curled it some this morning. She seemed to be doing well. It seemed to make her happy to get to know her mom again and share the kids with her. And that was important. Grant wanted that for Kallie, too.

"Yeah. I'm fine." He shrugged, deflecting her concern. "Just trying to get everything ready for training to start next week."

From the concern that pulled Kallie's brows together, he couldn't tell if she bought his story. "Do you need help with anything?"

"Just the grooming."

"Okay. Grant, are you sure there's nothing else?"

He shot a glance at the house. "You could've let me know you were giving the kids their first haircuts."

Kallie frowned. "You would've wanted to be there for that?"

"Well, sure. I missed all the other firsts."

She closed her eyes. "I'm sorry. I didn't think about it that way."

It was something they couldn't go back on, and that's what annoyed him the most. Again, missing out on something monumental in the kids' lives. His dad never cared about those things, but Grant did. "How long is your mom staying?"

"I told her she can stay as long as she wants. She doesn't really have anything to get back for. Her full-time job was caring for her ailing aunt, who passed away last week. She's really enjoying the kids and being back on the farm. And I'm enjoying getting to know her better."

Smiling, he couldn't begrudge her that. "I'm glad."

Seeing her happy like this strengthened his resolve to tell her about his new perspective. He no longer thought he could enjoy being a father while also being a bachelor. Now he wondered if he was actually missing out on something special. If he tried hard enough, could he convince Kallie that their relationship was worth another try?

After wolfing down a peanut butter sandwich, Grant found ways to keep busy in the barn, locating supplies Frank had stashed that Grant would need next week.

Dakota, Chief and Bella explored all the scents the barn had to offer while Grant hunted around. In one of the barn's side rooms, he was digging through a box when he heard scratching above his head.

What was that? He put the box away and stood to scan the rafters. Mice, maybe? Did he need to set traps?

"Oh, Grant," a voice said from the doorway. "Glad I found you."

He turned, putting off the rodent search for now. Edith watched him, arms crossed.

"Hey," he said, frowning. Had something happened with Kallie or the kids? "Everything okay?"

"Oh, fine. Fine. I just wanted to talk a few things through with you. I don't get much of a chance at the house, as you haven't been there very often."

Grant raised a brow. "Okay…"

"Listen," she said. "I've decided to hire someone to finish the farmwork for the rest of the summer."

He frowned. "You mean Kallie's decided?"

"I did, but ultimately, it doesn't matter who made the decision. It's my way of helping out around here."

"Well, we appreciate your interest in helping out, Edith, but it's not necessary. Kallie and I agreed to share the work."

"But plans change. Now that I'm here, you're relieved of your obligation."

Now both brows rose. "My obligation?"

"To the farm and to the kids. Now you're free to go teach your seminar classes, or join another nonprofit in Iowa, or whatever." She smiled, which sure felt patronizing. "Even if I don't hire someone, we still don't need your services anymore, because I can help with the kids while Kallie runs the farm."

Grant straightened, drawing his hands out of his pockets. "My time here is about more than farmwork."

"That may be true, but I think it's best for everyone if your time here ended soon."

"Now, hold it right there, ma'am. I don't mean any disrespect, but don't forget I own half of this land. And those are my kids we're talking about."

"Are you meaning to marry Kallie, then?" Edith stared him down over her crossed arms. "Because Kallie needs a husband."

Grant's frown deepened. "She said that?"

"She said she needs a dependable father for her children."

The words hit him square in the chest. A dependable father. Something his father wasn't. Was Grant not one, either?

"In my eyes," Edith said, "that includes being a husband. Because it's not enough to like your kids and show up whenever it's convenient. If you're living on this farm, and you're enjoying the benefits that Kallie provides for you, like a roof over your head and free food to eat, then you had better pull your own weight with those children. It's about committing to them *and* their mother."

"Okay, I'm going to stop you right there." You know, before he punched his fist through the barn wall. "You make me sound like some sort of bum, but you have no idea what I do around here. Everything is for Kallie and the kids. I'm trying to save this farm just as much as she is. That's why I'm in this barn right now instead of inside playing with Peter and Ainsley—getting ready for next week's training camp."

Edith didn't even flinch. "Is *that* why you're out here?"

"Yes."

"Not to pout about me being here? About you not being the big man on campus anymore?"

"Of course not." Though her words did sting a bit.

"And not because this training business is all about you rather than the farm?"

"Edith—"

"Because my Kallie is strong. She doesn't need some superhero flying in to save her from the situation she's been put in. Especially one who then abuses his privilege of being here. What my daughter needs is a partner who gives and sacrifices and commits. Things you never gave to her."

Wow. Hands balled into fists, Grant glued them to his sides. "I'm done talking about this with you. Now, get out of my barn. Whatever issues Kallie and I have, we'll discuss them together. Privately."

Edith's opinions on his relationship with Kallie weren't necessarily true. And neither was her assumption of his character. But man, her words cut into his confidence. He'd better make sure that what she'd said about him wasn't true.

One thing was clear. There was nothing Edith could say to convince him to give up his kids.

And if Kallie would accept him, he wasn't giving her up, either.

Saturday evening, Kallie, her mom and the kids finally made it home from their first farmers market of the year. Their vegetables still weren't ready to sell, but they had been sure to bake a bunch of pies, cookies and fresh bread to make up for it. And that had gone over wonderfully—better than she'd expected. Though her earnings were meager compared to some of the other vendors, who'd brought a wider variety of things to display, Kallie couldn't have been prouder of how well she'd done.

Her only regret was that Grant hadn't been there.

She'd hoped he could find time to join them. It had been an exciting day for her, and she'd wanted to share it with him. But the day had come and gone without him.

It was understandable, his absence. There was still a lot to do before the training camp started Monday morning. And ultimately, she was proud of him for working hard to earn money to save the farm.

But there was still that voice inside her, reminding her of his workaholic ways. His tendency to grab hold of a dream and lose sight of everything else. The worry that she was invisible.

Because if he'd truly known how important the day

was for her, he would have tried to make at least an appearance, right?

And it wasn't the first time he'd disregarded her wishes. Bringing a dog home, staying on the farm when she'd asked him to leave. Even starting this training business. Sure, he'd asked for her opinion first, but if he'd remembered and cared that she didn't want other dogs here, then he wouldn't have even brought it up.

After bringing everything inside and putting her money in a safe place where the kids wouldn't reach it, she went about starting supper. Mom hopped between helping her cook and occupying Ainsley and Peter.

Grant arrived just in time for supper, and this time he stayed to eat. A light drizzle outside pattered on the windows as they ate a fairly quiet supper. He did ask about how the farmers market went today, which lifted Kallie's spirits some.

"So, hey," he said, after supper was done and she was putting dishes in the dishwasher. He stood beside her at the sink while Mom was in the living room with the kids. "I found something in the barn that I want to show you."

"Oh yeah?"

"Yep. Finish your dishes and we'll head over there. That is, if your mom doesn't mind watching the kids for a little bit." He must have read concern on her face, because he added, "It's okay. We won't be gone long."

Raindrops dotted the windshield and body of the farm pickup parked in the earth-saturated turnaround. Dakota farmland stretched as far as the sunset-lit horizon, and a light sprinkle on their skin from clouds rolling in hinted at more rain to come.

"What's the surprise?"

"Shh, it's in the barn."

Kallie eyed Grant as he walked beside her. He kept his gaze trained forward, though she was certain he was hiding a playful grin.

"This had better be good, Mr. Young," she countered, "taking me away from washing dishes and all."

He didn't answer. Only let a twitch of his mouth indicate that smile again.

They entered the barn, and Kallie scanned the open space for anything out of place. But nothing suspicious jumped out.

"Grant, I—"

"Shh."

Kallie shut her mouth. Grant was heading for a side room and motioned with his head for her to follow. Quirking a brow, she did, again sweeping her gaze around for something amiss.

When they were inside the small room, he pointed up at the exposed rafters, where Dad had stored away old junk and supplies. He put a finger to his lips, and suddenly, she heard the soft, squeaky mewling of newborn kittens.

She couldn't contain her grin. "Where are they?" she whispered.

"On top of that door." Grant pointed to an old door suspended in the rafters. "She must have climbed the storage boxes over there and walked along the rafters to this spot. I can't see any other way she'd get up there."

"Clever mama."

"Mamas usually are." Grant gave her a wink before

leaving to grab the double-sided ladder, already set up in a corner.

He brought it back and motioned for her to climb one side. Grabbing hold, she stepped up each wrung until she could peek over the top of the rafters.

There it was, the little nest the barn cat had made on top of the door, tucked beside other various pieces of long-forgotten junk. Mama cat must have been off hunting, but she'd left behind four adorable, fuzzy kittens. Their squeaks and tiny bodies crawling over each other was enough to make Kallie giggle.

"How'd you find them?"

"I was in here looking for training supplies." Grant climbed the other side of the ladder and looked over the rafters, too, shooting her a wink that had her knees fixing to buckle.

"How did I miss these little guys being born?" Kallie asked. "They're so precious."

"It's been a busy few weeks. I'm not an expert on barn cats, but from what I can guess, they've only been up here a couple of weeks or so. I'm wondering if they were born while we were in Iowa."

"Oh, probably. Or right before we left." Had she honestly been that busy and preoccupied, to not notice a new batch of kittens?

Her arm brushed against his black checkered sleeve, only the ladder between them.

"Sorry," she murmured.

"It's fine." His voice came low and thick, bringing her gaze up.

Dark green and brown depths reached into her,

searching her as if he could take her all in. She didn't know what he'd find.

Then his hand covered hers and she pulled away. She took to climbing off the ladder, and he followed in long, swift strides. He reached the doorway before her, hand up against the frame, fencing her in.

Inches from him, she sensed his heat.

"You going to push me away forever, Kal?"

Her heartbeat stumbled. "What's that supposed to mean?"

His fierce eyes captured her. "Just tell me something. Do you ever regret us?"

Closing her eyes, Kallie felt her chest tighten. The look in Grant's eyes wounded her, his vulnerability matching hers completely. What could she possibly say that wouldn't change things between them?

Or maybe things had already changed.

Faint light crept through the open door, lighting the side of his square jaw, and suddenly she had to fight the urge to reach out and cup his cheek in her hand. Slowly, she shook her head. "No. I regret how we had the kids, that we didn't wait until we were married. But no, I don't regret us. At all."

The muscles in his jaw tightened. He bent his head, and his lips grazed hers before landing on them fully, sweeping her away. A long time coming, his kiss was sunshine and rain and harvest all wrapped up together. *Grant* was all those things. The blossoming of new romance intertwined with the deep current of old.

How she wanted to fall. But tears rushed against her closed eyes as she somehow managed to break the kiss and step out of his arms. "I—I just can't," she whispered, her voice broken by a sudden sob. "I'm sorry, I just can't."

She rounded him and fled toward the door.

"Why not, Kallie?" His voice followed her. "Are you afraid?"

Kallie spun and stared him down. Here she was, running again. She had to face her battles instead of burying them. A storm raged inside her as soft rain pattered outside the barn. What little moonlight remained had splashed across his features in the open door, highlighting the fierceness of his green-brown eyes.

"I can't imagine why anyone would want to be with me," she finally said, her voice catching again. Dumb tears. "Everyone wants to love the twins. And I'm the mean old monster who hid them for two years." She blinked and tears dropped down both cheeks. "What I did was unforgiveable."

His stare never wavered. "But I forgive you."

"I don't believe that." She paused for a moment. Then went on. "I can't make the past go away, Grant. It'll always be there, this incredibly dark shadow over our history. I think it's better that I be alone. I've been invisible my whole life—why change now?"

"Because maybe I want to be with you."

"You don't." She pursed her lips to stop their tremor. He had to stop this nonsense before it got worse. She already knew how this would end. If he didn't mess things up between them, she certainly would, given time. "You want to be with the kids, just like everyone else, and you're settling for me because we come as a package deal."

"That's not true."

"It is. You found out about the kids and you planted yourself here at the drop of a hat. But you wouldn't stay for me back then."

"Kal—"

"Is that not true? You're more devoted to the kids than to me."

He hesitated for only a second, and that was all the confirmation she needed. "It might have started out that way. I was angry and hurt. But I'm not the one to cast the first stone. I've hurt you, too, remember? Unfortunately, I think you're doing a pretty solid job of condemning yourself." His tone was even, matter-of-fact, and it sliced through her with precision. "You're not worried I won't forgive you. You're bitter because you haven't forgiven yourself."

Kallie shook. She pivoted and continued her trajectory toward the house. Rain splattered across her shoulders and hair, but it didn't matter. When she slipped inside, Ruby met her at the door. Kallie dropped to her knees and dug her fingers through Ruby's coat, allowing her to press her head into Kallie's shoulder. Moisture squeezed from Kallie's eyes.

*God, tell me it's going to be okay. Tell me it's all going to work out. I can't keep living like this.*

"Hun, are you okay?"

Mom stood in the doorway between the living room and kitchen, a knitting bag in her hands, as if she'd been occupying her time with that after the kids went down for bed.

When she saw Kallie's eyes, her features darkened. "What happened? Where's Grant?"

"It's fine," Kallie said. "It's not like that. I just... I don't know."

"Come in out of the doorway." Mom bustled into the kitchen. She placed her knitting bag on the table and went for a coffee mug. As Kallie sank into a kitchen chair at the table, Mom poured water from an already steaming kettle on the stove into a mug, then dropped in a bag of chamomile. She gently set it in front of Kallie. "Drink."

Her voice was hushed and soothing, like how Kallie imagined it would have sounded if she'd been nine and awakened in the middle of the night by a nightmare.

Mom sat across from her as Kallie lifted the mug and blew on the contents, the moist steam kissing her cheeks and the aroma filling her senses. Begging her to relax and lean into the comfort it offered.

"Everything's confusing, Mom. I don't know how I should think or feel, or what I should do. Nothing's made sense since—I don't even know." When was the last time she'd felt like she had a handle on life? Definitely not since Grant walked back into her life, and not since Dad passed away. But even before that, life was a mess. Had she been struggling for control and understanding and balance all of her life?

The woman across from her folded her hands. "What are you trying to figure out? Your feelings for Grant?"

Memories of his kiss and his wounded eyes brought forth a burn behind her eyes. "I suppose. Yes. I think so."

"Do you care about him?"

"I do. But how much, I don't know. Why does everything have to be complicated?" Sighing, she rubbed her hands over her face. "I just don't want to be hurt again."

"Well, I'm concerned about him, to be honest," Mom said. "He hasn't stopped by to see the kids much. And when he does stop in, he doesn't stay long. He's here but he's—distant. Are you sure you want a father like that for your kids?"

"Oh, no, he's a great dad." Kallie lowered her hands to her mug, never more sure of anything. "The kids already adore him."

Mom's brows drew together. "Oh?"

"He plays with them, feeds them, bathes them, puts them to sleep…he's even a big help around the house. Sometimes I can't keep him away. In fact, *most* of the time I can't."

"I didn't know. He's really that good with them?"

"Yeah," Kallie said, thinking on it more. "And I think this week he was giving you some space. You know, letting you meet the kids and reconnect with me."

"To be honest, Kallie, I thought he was a freeloader. I thought he was using you to get the land."

"What? Oh, no. He's nothing like that, Mom. He works very hard."

"But he left you when you were engaged."

"I—I know. And I'm still working through that." She met her mom's stare. "But no matter how he and I are, I know without a shadow of a doubt that he's an amazing dad to Peter and Ainsley. I wouldn't want any other for them."

Mom raised her brows at the strong statement, then dropped her gaze to her folded hands. "I'm…I'm glad. That's what those babies deserve."

"He's also the one who encouraged me to let you stay that first night. To figure this stuff out between us." She smiled. "I'm glad he did."

Concern etched further into Mom's face. She stood from the table and moved to the dishwasher.

She proceeded to unload it, and Kallie listened to the dishes clank together. "Are you okay?" When Mom didn't answer right away, Kallie leaned forward in her chair. "Mom?"

"I think I've made a big mistake."

Kallie stood. "What do you mean? What happened?"

When Mom turned to her, her thin brows were raised over apprehensive eyes. She brushed her ash-blond hair off her cheek. "I told Grant to leave the farm."

The words clanged around Kallie's brain like a penny dropped into a can. "You what?"

"I'm sorry. I honestly thought he was no good for you and that he was slacking on his commitment, so I told him to leave or ask you to marry him—"

"You told him *that*? Oh, Mom. When?"

"Late last night."

"Oh no." Kallie buried her face in her hands. "Mom, I don't need a husband. Or at least, not one that's, you know, twisted into marrying me."

"I didn't know what his intentions were."

"Well, I don't either, but…" Groaning, Kallie sank back in her chair. "This is such a mess."

Mom rubbed her hand on her opposite arm. "I'm sorry, hun. I only meant to fix things."

Was that why he'd kissed her tonight? Had Mom gotten to him, pressuring him to commit to her as much as to the kids? "Please don't do stuff like this in the future. I already have enough drama in my life raising twins, and trying to keep the farm going, and working out stuff with Grant. I don't need the waters muddier."

"I know. I'm very sorry."

Kallie shook her head. Was she being childish? She stood and joined her mom at the counter. "I don't mean to make you feel bad. I know you had the best of intentions." She reached for a clean plate and slid it into the cupboard. "I just need to figure this stuff out on my own." What had she been thinking, confiding in someone else about her worries and fears? Whenever she did stuff like that, it always turned around to bite her. "Stuff with Grant is messy, and I honestly don't know where it's going. Might be dead in the water already, after the argument we had tonight. But the last thing I want is someone who feels obligated to stay."

Her parents had had a loveless marriage in the end. She didn't want to leave that legacy for her kids, too.

As Kallie finished putting away the plates and moved on to the silverware, she realized, however, that she didn't want to leave behind a legacy of single parenthood, if she could help it. But it wasn't like a girl could count on a romantic relationship to fall into her lap.

Had she been too hard with Grant? Could they have developed an actual, long-lasting romance—before she'd ruined everything tonight? That is, if his actions tonight had not been influenced by Mom.

Kallie woke with a start. She rubbed her bleary eyes and blinked. What time was it? The sky was dark with rain but the house was too loud... Wait. Kallie listened closely, and she gasped when she finally strung together a coherent thought. The rainstorm that had started tonight. It wasn't raining now.

It was hail.

She stumbled from her bed and to the window, pulling back the curtain to squint into the yard. Hail hopped like white grasshoppers across the turnaround and her front yard.

Hail was a part of the farmer's life, a gamble taken against Mother Nature every year. But that didn't make it any easier to stand at her window and listen to it ruin the crop she still needed.

This year, it mattered more than most. If she didn't have that crop…

"God, please." She whispered the plea into the darkness. A tear slipped down her cheek and wet her collarbone. "Please let everything be okay."

# Chapter Nine

The next morning, Grant packed up the dogs in the truck and headed for the fields before breakfast. As he drove, he surveyed the ditches, the puddles that lay everywhere. Some even still carried a few hailstones, and the grasses looked like they'd been mowed over.

So much devastation. He couldn't believe it. What thrived yesterday was obliterated today. He scoffed. Kind of a metaphor for his life right now.

As he approached one of the fields, he noticed Kallie already there, standing in front of her truck, leaning a hip against the bumper to scrutinize the field. Blond hair pulled up in a ponytail. A canvas jacket over a navy hooded sweatshirt. He parked beside her and looked around as he got out.

She glanced at him as he settled against the front of his pickup. Offered him a tiny, polite, completely platonic smile. So he nodded back.

"Called the insurance company from the cottage," he said, the only other sound being the breeze brushing over the ruined field. "They'll send an adjuster out soon."

"Great. Thanks for calling them."

"Yep."

Silence fell between them as he searched for more words. Juxtaposed to this morning's devastation, last night's argument seemed so far away, and yet it also seemed closer than ever. He was still reeling, still stunned at the way she'd spoken to him. It'd taken everything in him to keep from going back to the cottage and packing his bag. She obviously didn't love him and probably never would. Maybe he wasn't so sure about his feelings, either.

The only reason he'd stayed was to be there for the kids. He still wasn't his dad.

"I checked the corn," Kallie said.

"Yeah?"

"It doesn't look amazing, but it's still young. My guess is it'll bounce back." She folded her arms against her chest and turned her attention back to the wheat field in front of them. "This field looks terrible. Just like all the others I've checked today. All that money, gone. Just like that, in a matter of hours. And there's nothing we can do."

"I'm glad we got the insurance," he said.

"Me, too."

If they hadn't picked up that insurance, there would have been zero money coming back. Paying off their hefty agricultural loan without help from insurance or from a good harvest would have completely ruined them.

"Maybe we'll still make some profit," he said, "because of the insurance check."

"Oh, no. Grant, that's not how hail insurance works." Kallie shook her head, making brief eye contact with him before looking out to the field again. "These fields look bad, but I've seen far worse over the years. Honestly, my guess is that they're not completely destroyed. And if that's the case, we'll still have to harvest what we can."

"Wouldn't that be a good thing?"

"No, it could be worse. If the claims adjuster deems some of our wheat fields salvageable, then he'll only pay us back for the initial amount we put in. Which means we'll only be able to pay back that particular loan with this crop—with nothing left over for Dad's other bills. We'd have to use whatever we get out of the harvest to try to cover his other bills."

"Which won't be much because the surviving wheat won't be stellar after a hailstorm," Grant finished, understanding.

"Right."

Grant asked God for the thousandth time why this had to happen to them this year. Of all years, when they were trying their hardest to keep the land. "What's our next move?"

"We'll have to hustle if we want to plant something fast-growing here, to try to make up some of the difference. Not a great plan, and there's cost involved, but it's possible. After that, we'll have to rely on our corn's harvest, though that won't be ready until November, and many of our loans are due before then."

Awesome. Grant exhaled. "Adding insult to injury, the hail has also ruined a lot of our pheasant coverage. I checked that out before coming here, and it's pretty awful. We may not be able to do our training here like we'd planned. Or we'll have to simulate the training with dummies instead of birds, or pay to bring birds in." Which meant delaying their start a little, because he'd have to order those things. He'd debated over what to tell his clients ever since the hail started last night.

Kallie closed her eyes. "I shouldn't have been so stubborn trying to hold on to this place."

Had he heard her right? Grant looked to Kallie. "Hey, now. It's not your fault. You can't control the weather. We'll just do the best we can."

"I don't know. We should probably just sell. I don't see how we'll be able to pay our loans. Why don't we just cut our losses? Dad's memory is in our hearts anyway, not in the land."

Did she actually mean that? Grant tried to gauge her expression, but she just looked bone weary. Though also serious.

He tried to imagine what it would be like to sell the land and what it would mean for the kids. Would they have nothing to inherit after everything was said and done? And would Kallie lose a big piece of her heart in the process?

Kallie pushed off from the bumper and rounded the truck. "I'll call a real estate agent today."

"We don't have to move that fast," he said. "At least wait to hear what the insurance guy says."

She didn't answer, only climbed into her truck and shut the door. Didn't look at him as she backed out onto the road and drove back to the house. Classic Kallie, trying to keep it together.

Would she ever let down her guard and allow herself to become vulnerable?

* * *

Mom offered to get groceries this time, so she'd left Kallie alone in the house with the kids. Peter had been acting extra tired today and only wanted to be held. It all made sense when she checked his temperature and it was a low-grade fever. Good thing she hadn't needed to be anywhere today but on her recliner.

She'd taken Grant's advice about waiting to call a real estate agent, but she wasn't sure how long she could hold out. He'd told her they'd do their best to pay off the loans without giving up the legacy Dad had left behind. But Kallie had already done her best—and failed.

What else could she possibly do? Saving the farm was next to impossible. The promise of the kids' inheritance was fading into nothing.

But selling… She'd said the words to Grant, but didn't know if she'd truly meant them. Dad's memory was everywhere out here. It felt like he was still around, as long as she was on the farm. What if Dad's memory faded if she sold and moved away?

She might not have a choice.

Just then, a knock sounded at the door. Kallie glanced at the clock. Nearly five. Peter snuggled deeper into her shoulder, his forehead warm, as she opened the door and found Harvey Leese, her attorney, on the porch.

"Oh, hi, Harvey. I didn't miss a meeting, did I?"

"No, Kallie, nothing like that." Harvey smiled a little. "Just have another piece of mail to give you." He held out an envelope.

Kallie's eyes widened. "What do you mean?" She looked at him for an explanation, and his eyes filled with sympathy.

"Your dad wanted me to wait a couple of weeks after Grant Young started working here before giving you this note. He wanted 'the dust to settle a little,' or at least, that's what he told me."

Harvey chuckled. He'd known Dad as a good friend and not simply a client. "I could have mailed it, but I was traveling out of town, past this area anyway, and I figured you'd want to see it as soon as possible."

"Yes, thank you. I can't wait to open it."

"I'll leave you to it, then." Harvey touched the brim of his hat. "Have a good night."

He went out into the evening, sun setting around him. Kallie watched as he got into his SUV and drove away. Then she looked at the note.

Dad had written her one last time before passing away. A priceless gift she never could have imagined.

Peter whimpered on her shoulder. "It's okay, punkin." She checked his temperature and found it climbing, so she administered the appropriate amount of baby pain reliever to him. She wet a thin washcloth in the sink, then nestled into the recliner with Peter tucked close before draping the cloth across his little forehead. He seemed to appreciate it, judging by the quieting of his moans.

When he appeared as content as he'd get, she opened the envelope of Dad's letter.

Inside, she found two folded notes, one addressed to Mom in typed letters with the phrase "Give this note to your mom" typed below it, and one to Kallie in Dad's shaky handwriting.

The sight of his handwriting about did her in. She unfolded the letter and simply stared for a while, letting her tears blur the words. It was like holding his hand again, hearing his voice, watching him smile.

> *Dear Kallie Bug,*
> *You are the light of my life. My precious girl.*
>     *I want you to understand something. By now, you've seen my will, the request that you and Grant own the farm together. But what you may not understand is why.*
>     *As the sole owner of the farm, you have your hands full. And the twins are growing bigger and more active every day. I don't want you running it alone. But even more than the farm, I don't want you to be alone. Grant is the kids' father, and I've respected your wishes to keep silent on letting him know about the kids. However, I've come to realize it's too important of an issue not to be resolved.*
>     *So if you won't do it, I'll help the matters along myself. I hope you'll forgive me for that.*
>     *But when I ended my marriage to your mother, I made the biggest mistake of my life. I should have fought for us, not turned into a coward and let her slip away. I loved your mother, but I was hurt. That was no excuse. You suffered the most from my mistake, and for that, I'm truly sorry...*

The phone rang, interrupting her reading. She glanced at the doorway leading into the kitchen, then back at Peter, who was beginning to fall asleep. She really should get some cordless phones for the house.

Maybe she'd let it go to voicemail.

After a few rings, the voicemail switched on. Kallie rubbed her hand on Peter's back, thankful Ainsley was sleeping soundly upstairs.

"Hello," the voice said into the room. "This is Officer Craig Dunn of the Broken Bow Police Department, and I'm trying to reach Kallie Shore."

Kallie's heart dropped. She popped from her chair and sped to the phone.

"Yes, I'm here." Her voice was breathless in the receiver. "What's wrong?"

"Ma'am, there has been an accident involving your mother, Edith Shore—"

Kallie nearly dropped the phone. The rest of the conversation, the instructions, the details, were a blur as Kallie grappled with the news. Her mother had been in a car accident and was now in Broken Bow, the closest town with a decent hospital.

Kallie shook her head. "I'll be there as soon as I can. Thank you." She hung up the phone, then immediately picked it up again and punched in the cottage's number.

"Hello?"

"Grant, can you come over here?" The breath squeezed from Kallie's lungs.

"What happened?"

He could always tell. She closed her eyes. "It's my mom." She relayed the information the officer had told her. Or at least what she could remember of it. "Could you please—"

"I'm on my way," he said, then hung up the phone.

Kallie whispered a prayer of thanks, then hung up the phone, too. Peter started to cry, so she took off the cloth and wet it again. She was tempted to check his temperature, but it hadn't been very long since last time she'd checked. Instead, she made a new bottle with trembling hands, a prayer for her mom never far from her lips.

She tried to comfort Peter by tucking a bottle into his mouth. As she did, she heard the door open. Before she could even fully turn around, Grant was in the room and had slid her and Peter into his arms.

It was just what she needed to lose what little wall of fortitude she'd managed to cobble together in the past few minutes.

"Dear God," Grant whispered, Kallie tucked against his chest, "please protect Edith. Thank You for preserving her life, and please help Kallie know Your bravery and comfort. We know You are a God who loves His children. We are amazed at Your faithfulness even when times don't make sense. Give us that peace and understanding. In Jesus's name, I pray. Amen."

Kallie pressed her forehead to Grant's shoulder before drawing back. "Thank you."

"Here, give me Peter." As he took his son in his arms, Grant bore his green-brown stare into Kallie, filling her with strength. "Are you okay driving?"

She nodded. "Yes, I can do it."

"Do you need me to do anything for you?"

"No, thanks. Except Peter has a fever. The thermometer is on the table there. You just put it to his temple and press a button…it's kind of weird…"

"It's all right, Kallie. I can look it up online if need be. Go. I've got it covered."

Kallie backed to the door, grabbing her keys off the nail. "You might need to give him a bath, and Ainsley is asleep upstairs."

"I've got this, Kallie. Go."

His words were firm, but they filtered through her like soft, warm oil over aching muscles and joints. She nodded. Grant really did have everything under control, and she really could let him help.

She raced out to the pickup and started it up. "Thank You, God, for Grant," she whispered, then drove out of the turnaround and down the gravel road toward Broken Bow Memorial Hospital.

Grant sat at his kitchen table, empty coffee mug in hand, staring at the little window above his sink at the moonlight splashing across the counter and kitchen floor.

He didn't feel right sitting here. He should be with Kallie and his kids.

While at her house, he'd fed both kids their bottles on his lap while searching the internet on Kallie's computer for what to do with a nearly fourteen-month-old with a fever. Then Grant had bathed Peter and put him to bed in the lightest pajamas he could find, as his temperature was at one hundred. Everything had gone pretty well, all things considered.

Kallie had been gone for the entire evening, finally returning around nine. She'd seemed weary, ready to sleep. Because of the position in which the paramedics had found Edith's car, and the fact that she couldn't seem to keep anything down, they'd been concerned that she had carbon monoxide poisoning and possibly a concussion. They'd kept her overnight for observation.

Kallie wanted to be there at eight the next morning

to be available when the doctors made their rounds, so Grant was to come back no later than seven.

Well, here it was 1:00 a.m., and he'd still yet to leave the table. Why, he hadn't even removed his boots yet. Chief, Bella and Dakota had ignored their beds, too, going to sleep at his feet.

*God, I should be with my family, not sitting here in this cottage.*

He gritted his teeth, then stood. Plunked his coffee mug on the tabletop, and the dogs lifted their heads.

"I'm heading over there," he muttered. "At least to see if there are lights on, if they're doing okay." Peter had been a mite restless when he'd gone to bed, and Kallie had been so tired.

In the darkness, he walked over. As he approached the house, he didn't see any lights on. Best to circle the house, though, and make sure. Especially since the living room was in the back.

Halfway around, he spotted a lamp's soft glow and movement through one of the living room windows. The rocking recliner.

Kallie was awake.

He started for the door, then remembered Ruby. She wouldn't be quiet about someone coming through the door. So, he went back to the window nearest Kallie and rapped on it lightly with his knuckle. The recliner stopped. He waved and pointed to the door. Thankfully, there was a lot of moonlight, because Kallie seemed to recognize him. She rose from the recliner as if heading to the door to let him in.

She met him there, Ruby beside her. Grant gave Ruby's ears a quick scratch as he entered the kitchen.

"What are you doing here?" Kallie whispered. "Is something wrong?"

"No, no. I just came to check on you guys." A quick glance around told him things were a little hectic after he left. A container of formula sat open on the counter, dishes in the sink instead of in the dishwasher—Kallie's pet peeve, if he'd learned anything about her in the past few weeks—and the diaper bag's contents spilled across the table.

Peter fussed, and Grant swiveled his gaze back to Kallie. "Here, let me take him."

"Grant—"

"You need to sleep." He closed the space between them and gently slid his hands under Peter's head and body. Grant raised his brows at the heat coming off his son's skin.

Peter wriggled and fussed louder. "He won't sleep lying down," Kallie said, taking the opportunity to run a rag under the water. "That's why we're rocking."

"I can do that, Kallie. You need to sleep."

"No more than you do."

"You've been running hard, and you have to be up early tomorrow."

"I'm just wetting this rag."

And then what? No doubt finding another thing to do to take care of Peter, rather than relinquishing control.

Grant tucked his son into his shoulder, and though the boy moaned in discomfort from his fever, he seemed to quiet some at the change in position and seemed to realize who held him.

Stopping her from wringing out the rag, Grant gently stepped between her and the sink, placing his free hand on her arm. He dipped his head, seeking her face. "Hey," he said, his voice low.

Slowly, her eyes flitted up to meet his. Actually vulnerable this time. And transparent. And so very tired. Kallie was a survivor, plain as day. She constantly fought for her kids, but even more so, she fought to maintain mental equilibrium.

"I've got this," he murmured. His hand moved up her arm and cupped her cheek. She stiffened at his touch, but he held his ground until he felt her begin to relax into his touch. "You kill it every day for these kiddos. It's time you allowed someone to take care of you, too."

He ran his thumb on her cheek, and she closed her eyes, her brows knit as her beautiful mouth pressed together. Her chin trembled—for just an instant.

But it was enough.

He gently tugged her closer and placed a gentle kiss on her forehead. The scent of her hair and the feel of her soft skin nearly undid him, more than he ever could have realized was possible. "Go get some rest," he whispered against her skin. "I'll take the next shift."

He stepped back and her shoulders sank. All she did was nod before dropping the wet cloth on the counter and turning away.

She made it to the doorway between the kitchen and living room before pausing. "You'll check with me if you need anything, right?"

"Yes. If common sense and Google can't figure it out, then I'll wake you. Promise."

Nodding, she seemed to accept that before heading to bed upstairs.

"Okay, bud," Grant whispered, turning his atten-

tion to the little boy, who seemed to be getting a fit-
ful snooze on his shoulder. "Let's get you back in the
recliner."

He was certainly an oven, that little guy. Grant settled into the recliner, noticing all kinds of supplies surrounding it—thermometer, diapers and wipes, burp
cloths, medicine bulb syringe—even food bars. Basi-
cally anything he could need for the entire night, within
arm's reach.

Peter fussed and writhed. "Shh, shh… It's all right,
bud." He located a bottle of water on the end table, ready
to be filled with the portioned-out vial of formula sitting beside it. Snuggling Peter in one arm, he mixed up
the bottle and then put it to Peter's lips.

The boy drank eagerly, as if begging for any mea-
sure of comfort. Poor guy. He checked the medication
schedule Kallie had penciled out, which was also on
the end table. Looked as if nothing more could be administered for another three hours. Gently, he rocked
Peter forward and back, the slight creak of the recliner
soothing them both.

*God, please help Peter heal quickly.*

Grant closed his eyes and rocked for a while, listening to the near silence and hoping Kallie was getting
some sleep upstairs. It would probably be a long night
as Peter might not sleep well. Grant may need to be
creative in how to fill the time, if he himself couldn't
find sleep.

His mind wandered to the training camp starting
Monday. He'd been thinking through some ideas of how
to make it work, and now was probably as good a time

as any to browse the internet on his phone for answers to his questions.

He glanced at Peter. The boy's eyes were closed, and he sucked away on his bottle with decreasing fervor, as if he were falling asleep. Grant picked up the phone he'd deposited on the end table and opened the internet app.

As he researched, he was drawn further in by more questions and sought out more answers. Certain options seemed more feasible than others in fixing the problems he faced, but nothing seemed like a clear-cut winner. Everything would cost more money, more resources and more time. No matter how he looked at it, there was going to be struggle. Was setting up his own business the best way to go?

Peter shifted in his arms and started to fuss, pulling Grant's attention back to the moment. Peter dropped the bottle and it ran down Grant's leg and out into the middle of the living room, stopping just short of Ruby, who slept nearby.

Grant put his phone back on the end table, mid-search. "Shh, shh, it's okay." He whispered the words and helped Peter reposition onto his shoulder so he could burp. Guilt poked at him. How long had Peter laid there asleep, needing to burp, sucking in air from an empty bottle? Grant had been so focused on the research that he wasn't sure.

After seeing that Peter was good and satisfied, Grant tried to rock him some more. It took lots of fidgeting and fussing before Peter finally found a spot that seemed to work.

As Grant repositioned the damp cloth on Peter's head, the phone vibrated.

An email.

Strange, getting one so late at night. He figured it must have been junk but when he opened his inbox, he realized it was from a guy named Todd Dunmore, owner of Midwestern Game Outfitters. It was a huge operation in North Dakota that offered all levels of training for dogs and their handlers.

It was the most esteemed training facility in the Midwest, and Grant had dreamed of working there for years. He'd finally secured a couple of weekend clinics last winter in partnership with their full-time trainer, but then he hadn't heard from them since.

Grant opened the email.

Mr. Young,

Due to unforeseen circumstances, Midwestern Game Outfitters is now in need of an on-site trainer to work with our clients and hold regularly scheduled classes. This is a full-time position. You did excellent work while you were here, and we were highly impressed. We would like to consider you for this job. If interested, please reply with your resume to this email as soon as possible, along with a list of your ideas for where you envision taking our program.

Thank you,

Todd Dunmore

Midwestern Game Outfitters, founder

"Whoa," Grant whispered. He set his phone on the end table and rocked, allowing his gaze to meander around the room. Though it continually returned to his phone.

Was this new job opportunity the answer he'd been looking for? Kallie had said so herself that they were going to lose the land if they didn't sell. Maybe they were supposed to start a new life together in North Dakota.

Sure, he'd been concerned about how Kallie felt about him, but maybe he'd overreacted. Perhaps he'd moved too fast last night, because today, things seemed a little better. If they did have to go through the painful process of selling off Frank's land—something neither of them wanted—would she be willing to look to Grant as a member of their family and come with him to this new job?

The dream would look different than either of them had imagined—but what would it matter if they could be financially sound while starting over as a family?

He reached for his phone to reply to the message. As he typed, his mind whirled with ideas. And the more ideas he had, the more excited he grew at the possibility of going to North Dakota. But not alone—never alone. The kids and Kallie would need to be with him, and that would make his situation perfect. Maybe they could even purchase a spread of land somewhere outside town, so the kids could still enjoy growing up experiencing country life. They could start a new legacy to pass on from generation to generation.

After adding a few more ideas, he sent his email, making sure to say he'd send the resume tomorrow, as it was on his laptop at the cottage.

Peter had fallen asleep, mouth agape on Grant's arm. Hopefully they could both catch some shut-eye now. Though Grant wasn't sure his anticipation would let go of him anytime soon. Hope and purpose bloomed in his chest. This plan might actually work.

With the house still asleep and early-morning light sifting through the main level curtains, Kallie crept down the stairs. She'd slept much longer than she'd meant to—had only planned to get in an hour or two but had instead slept until six. How had Grant fared through the night?

Reaching the last step, she silently poked her head around the corner.

Grant and Peter were on the recliner. Steady breathing told her they were sleeping, Peter on Grant's chest with his pudgy arm tucked under his chin. Her heart swelled with pride as she slipped across the carpet toward the kitchen.

The buzzing of Grant's phone alerted her. She turned. It continually buzzed as if someone was calling, but Grant didn't move. However, Peter did begin to squirm.

Kallie padded to the phone and picked it up, intending to silence it so it wouldn't wake Peter. When she looked at the screen, she paused. The number was from North Dakota. Who did Grant know there?

She shook her head. It was probably a training client. He had those all over the country—or at least used to, before he canceled all of those appointments to stay here with the kids. The call quit, and she turned the volume down to silent. But as she was about to set down the phone, an email popped up on the screen.

Honestly, Kallie hadn't planned to look at it. But when words like "Follow-Up Request for Interview" popped up, she had to stare.

A job interview? He was going to leave?

Kallie stared at him, sleeping on the recliner with his son, who was so small and vulnerable and relied entirely on his parents. How could Grant think of leaving when he'd been so adamant about staying before? She couldn't believe he'd actually grown tired of being a dad, letting his old restlessness for the farm influence his decisions again. And right after the hailstorm's devastation, too.

He might as well have kicked her in the stomach. She placed his phone down and hurried into the kitchen. She needed to leave if she wanted to speak with the doctor before picking up her mom.

She wrote out a quick note for Grant telling him she'd left, then grabbed a food bar and the bag of clothes she'd packed for Mom before hurrying out to her truck. Her thoughts centered on him as she drove, how he'd popped into her life so fully after a two-year dry spell where she'd been convinced he'd never return. She'd hoped a few weeks of his dedication would be enough time to trust that he'd stay here for good, but now she could see that wasn't the case.

By the time Kallie had driven the forty-five miles to Broken Bow, where the hospital was located, she'd cried all her tears. She hoped her face didn't look too red and swollen as she turned into the parking and trekked up to her mom's room. She now knew where Grant's heart lay, and it wasn't with the farm, with the kids, or with her.

Mom was awake and alert when Kallie stepped in, a much-improved state over yesterday.

"Did you sleep, Mom?"

"Oh, a little. You know hospital beds," Mom laughed softly. "I'm ready to leave, though."

"Well, I brought you some clothes." Kallie held up the plastic sack she carried. "We'll have you heading home in no time."

The smile that lit Mom's face was full of hope, and it brightened Kallie's weary heart, too. Being with Mom really was like going home. Sure, there was more hurt to heal. But Kallie was certain they were well on their way.

When the doctor said everything looked good, they headed for the truck.

"Mom?" Kallie asked as they drove home. "What happened with the accident? How'd you hit that embankment?"

Mom sighed. "Well, I had a lot on my mind, and one of my grocery bags tipped over on the passenger seat, so I reached for it, not really thinking. I suppose that was it."

Kallie glanced Mom's direction. "You had a lot on your mind?"

"Yeah, but it was nothing."

"Enough to make you run into an embankment."

"I told you, that was the groceries' doing." Another sigh escaped Mom, and she turned to the window.

Hmm. Maybe Kallie's lack of communication skills was inherited.

"Mom. I can tell you're thinking about something. What's going on?"

"It's really nothing."

"I'm not sure I believe that."

"I was trying to decide if I should stick around, all right?"

Kallie nearly veered toward the highway's shoulder. Instead, she gripped her steering wheel tightly and threw her mom a hard stare. "You want to leave?"

Her focus dropping to her hands, Mom frowned. Her chin trembled before she regained control of it. "Not because I *want* to. I was thinking about my conversation with Grant and then with you, and how my attempt at helpfulness was actually a hindrance."

Maybe it hadn't been a hindrance after all. But Kallie kept the thought to herself. She knew she needed to talk to Grant, even if everything inside her screamed for her to sweep it under the rug and just ask him to leave.

The occasional tree passed on either side of the highway. Not a lot of those out on the prairie. Kallie waited for her mom to continue.

"I missed that time in your life. Young romance. When boys are chasing you, and I get to send them off." A wry smile crawled up Mom's face. "And I'm coming to realize you're a grown woman now. You don't need anyone doing that for you. I'm sorry I didn't see it."

"Mom, just because I'm a grown woman doesn't mean I don't need you."

"No, I know." She seemed to be weighing her thoughts. "But it's time for me to find my role in life. Get a job somewhere and plug back into society." Her eyes sparkled. "Don't worry. I'll be back to visit. You can't get rid of Grandma that easily." She met Kallie's gaze. "Can't get rid of *Mama* that easily, either."

Kallie smiled, her heart warming. It was a blessing to be remembered. "Oh, I have a letter for you. It's from Dad."

"Your dad?" Mom's eyes rounded. "He wrote to me?"

"The attorney just gave it to me yesterday, along with a note for me." Keeping her eyes on the road, she slipped it from her purse and handed mom's note over.

"In the craziness of last night, I didn't even get a chance to finish reading mine."

Mom pressed the note to her heart, then held it in her lap. "Thank you. I'll read it later—when I can soak it in."

Kallie nodded. "Totally get that." She'd be doing the same with hers.

Her phone rang.

She glanced at it and frowned. "It's Grant." Answering it, she stuck it between her ear and shoulder. "Hello?"

"Kallie, we're at the ER in Broken Bow." His voice sounded matter-of-fact, but that didn't stop Kallie's heart rate from spiking. "Peter's fever continued to climb, so we came in. It's coming back down now, but just wanted to give you a heads-up."

A heads-up that her baby was in the emergency room? Kallie pulled off at a gravel road and turned the truck back toward Broken Bow. "We'll be there in ten minutes."

She hung up and dropped the phone in her lap, then gripped the wheel with white knuckles.

"What's going on?" Mom asked.

"Peter's in the ER for his fever. Grant said it kept going up."

"Oh, Lord, watch over that sweet baby," Mom whispered, sitting back against the passenger seat.

"Sorry to cart you back into town, Mom. I know I'm supposed to get you home to rest—"

"Don't think on it a second longer," Mom reassured, placing a hand on Kallie's knee. "I'm fine. It won't hurt me in the slightest to go home a little later than we'd planned."

Kallie closed her eyes for the instant she could allow herself to before returning her focus to the road. All she wanted to do was find Peter and Ainsley, whisk them away to some protected place and hold them close. It had taken a lot for her to give up control and let Grant help her with caring for the kids. But she knew this to be true—she should have been the one there for Peter when he needed her most. That was a mother's job, and she'd completely missed the mark.

# Chapter Ten

❧

"Right in here."

Grant looked up as an ER nurse opened the examination room door and let Kallie inside.

It was a small room with an exam table in the middle and various instruments attached to the walls surrounding it. One chair sat near the door, but Kallie zeroed in on the table, where Peter and Ainsley sat on Grant's lap. He had his phone out, showing them videos of themselves. Ainsley beamed and was pointing at the screen, while Peter had snuggled into Grant's chest, watching the screen with a stoic expression, as if he might fall asleep.

Kallie dropped her purse on the chair and made her way around the side of the table. She kissed Ainsley's head before lifting Peter out of Grant's arms.

He watched her as she eyed Ainsley, who was glued to the video. Guilt poked him. Kallie didn't like the kids to get screen time. He cleared his throat. "Sorry, I didn't know we'd be in here so long. I didn't have anything else for them to do and they were getting bored."

She didn't say anything. Only turned her attention to their son and cradled him closer. "Hi, punkin. Everything's all right."

"Where's your mom?"

"In the pickup, waiting. What's his temperature now?"

"He's reading at 102-point-something. They gave him something to bring the fever down. We're waiting on test results."

Kallie's eyes widened. "Tests? For what?"

"Lots of things. Trying to make sure they understand what's causing the fever."

Exhaling, she began to pace. "This is my fault. I should have done something to prevent this from happening."

"It wasn't your fault."

"If I'd been up with him all night, maybe I could have done something. I could have called the hospital and told them I'd pick Mom up later than planned. Or brought the kids with me—"

"Kallie, enough. Don't beat yourself up. You did everything right."

He was the one who'd done everything wrong.

If he hadn't been paying so much attention to his pursuits last night, maybe he would've caught Peter's rising fever before it got too high.

All morning in the ER, he'd mulled over Edith's words to him the other day.

*Kallie needs a dependable father to her children.*

*This training business is all about you rather than the farm.*

And on both counts, she was right. In so many ways,

he'd let his quest to become a successful, opposite-of-his-own-father dad get in the way of what was most important. He'd focused too much on self-achievement rather than on connecting with his kids—the whole reason he was out here in the first place.

Peter and Ainsley needed a dependable father—one who wouldn't set them aside to achieve his own goals. He'd fallen short of that standard.

Fussing, Peter pulled himself closer to Kallie's chest, grabbing hold of her shirt with his strong yet tiny hands. He needed his mother, and she'd been right this whole time in not giving up control. No one knew these kids like she did. And no matter how Grant tried, he wasn't sure he could catch up and become the father they needed.

Kallie watched their son, her brows low over her eyes. "If anything happened to him while I'd taken a break," she mumbled, "I'd never be able to forgive myself."

"You really know how to kick a guy when he's down."

"I only meant—"

"I know what you meant. That you don't trust me to care for our kids, and you probably don't trust anyone to do that job but yourself."

Her eyes flashed. "Is that so wrong? As far as I'm concerned, I'm the only trustworthy one around here."

His defenses rose. "Um, does keeping the kids a secret for two years ring a bell?"

"Does applying for a job in North Dakota?"

She flung the words so hard at him, he had to jerk back. "You saw my email?"

"And I'm glad I did, too, because now I know where your allegiance is. It's with me, myself and I, and we're just a part of your plans if it's convenient."

A knock on the door interrupted them and a nurse stepped in. The man glanced between Grant and Kallie. "Sorry, am I interrupting something?"

"No," they said in unison.

"Okay. Well, we got the test results back," he said, folding his arms and leaning against the wall.

Thankfully, it wasn't any of the major illnesses or infections they'd tested for. It was only a virus that would run its course over the next couple days. They were free to take Peter home.

Outside the hospital, the sun shone brightly and the birds sang in the nearby cottonwoods, but a storm brewed in Grant's chest worse than a ravaging hailstorm. Kallie, with Peter on one hip, strode a few steps ahead of him.

"Kal, I was looking into a job that was offered to me out of the blue."

"That makes it so much better. Thanks."

Sighing, he glanced at the sky. "I'd hoped we'd all go up there together."

She whirled to face him. "And what? Leave my dad's farm like it meant nothing to us?"

"I only sent in my application because you said we were selling."

"Who said we're selling the farm? I know I mentioned it as a *possibility*, but I was also speaking out of frustration. You should have talked to me about it."

"Like that would have made any difference." He approached, wishing he had any idea of what Kallie was thinking half the time. "No one jumps around here without asking you how high. Wouldn't matter what I wanted or what I thought was best for the family because we're not a partnership like we're supposed to be."

"You're right about that." She tossed him her keys. "You're taking my pickup home. I'm taking your truck so I can have the kids with me."

Grant narrowed his eyes. "Are you serious?"

The glare he received in reply caused him to shut his mouth. Kallie retrieved her mom, and then they all climbed into his truck. Grant loaded Ainsley into her car seat, then took Kallie's set of keys back across the parking lot in the direction of Kallie's pickup. Alone.

He'd thought he'd known how the future would play out. Had tried to make the right decisions. But in the end, nothing was like he'd planned, and he'd lost it all.

So much for starting over as a family.

After Mom went to bed, Kallie stepped outside. An evening rain had stopped, at least for now, and everything smelled clean with promise. So opposite from the feelings of defeat and betrayal weighing down her heart right now.

Kallie draped an old work sweatshirt across the damp porch step and sat down on it. Ruby rested beside her, her coppery ears and white head resting against Kallie's arm. Hugging her knees, Kallie scanned the turnaround beneath the flood lamp attached to the barn across the way. Everything was quiet and still.

Suddenly, Ruby sat up, her ears perked. Then Kallie heard the quick padding of dog steps across gravel. Chief and Bella appeared in the circle of lamplight, and Ruby's tail wagged back and worth, whapping into the bottom step. Obviously on a mission, Grant's dogs sniffed and explored at quick speed, not stopping too long on any particular spot.

Then footsteps, and Grant strode into the light, holding Dakota's leash. He hadn't seen Kallie yet, or at least he kept walking like he hadn't. When he paused in the middle of the turnaround, probably allowing his dogs the space to look around, Kallie took the moment to observe him. Tall, with square shoulders and trim build. Hands in his jeans pockets beneath a gray hooded sweatshirt. Signature baseball cap pulled low. Looked really good—in some ways, like home. Which was dangerous, because home was something he'd never be.

Ruby couldn't stand it any longer, so Kallie gave in and used her release word. Ruby cut across the turnaround to join Bella and Chief in their exploration. She ran directly across Grant's path, only pausing long enough to give Dakota a minor sniff.

Grant spotted her, and Kallie froze. After a couple of seconds, he made his slow way over.

"Taking your dogs out one last time before bed?" she asked, breaking the silence.

"Yep."

With lamplight behind him, she couldn't make out his face or what he was feeling. But judging by how the past couple days had gone, chances were he wasn't feeling the greatest.

Grant shifted. "So, I'm going to move into town. It'll give your mom a place to live that's her own. Besides that, I think it's better this way for you and me."

The finality of his words chopped like a guillotine.

Like she'd suddenly been uprooted and left there to flail. But wasn't that what she'd expected him to do all along? Wasn't it what she wanted?

She swallowed her tears. "Fine. And what about your North Dakota job?"

He shrugged. "Told you I'm not leaving the kids, so…"

She huffed, her anger sinking deeper into her heart. Didn't really answer her question. Did that mean he wasn't going, or that he was going to seek custody and try to take the kids with him?

Her head hurt. What a mess this whole thing had turned out to be.

"For what, a couple of hours here and there? I thought we agreed it'd be best for you to be on the premises to see them as much as possible."

"Well, you're sure making it clear I'm not wanted here, Kal. So which is it?"

"Thanks for letting me move my work out here for the time being, Maxwell." Grant surveyed the kennels that were already built and the open space ready for the dogs to run. He'd had to postpone the dog training another week, but thankfully, his client was still willing and able to bring all three dogs, this time to Maxwell Thornton's land just outside Bitter Creek. "And how great that your spread was spared from the storm. It'll be full of birds in time for hunting season."

"Storms are weird things," Maxwell said. "I think we were right on the cusp of it. Got our roof a little in town, but nothing damaging out here. Sorry about your place, though. Anything we can do to help?"

Hands in pockets, Grant shuffled a foot, nudging a rock. "Thanks. But we'll manage."

It'd been a week since the ER visit and Grant's move into town. He'd been out to the farm every day to see the kids like he'd promised, and Kallie had always conveniently made herself scarce during that time. Except for this morning, when she was there to tell him that the insurance adjuster had come by. He'd deemed the field only 60 percent ruined—which meant they still needed to see what they could salvage and sell that less-than-awesome wheat.

She'd also told him she was selling off a portion of the land.

Though she'd offered to split the profits, he'd declined. She and the kids needed that money more than he did. Besides, most of what he made was going to go toward Frank's loans, child support and the kids' college funds. It would've circled around anyway.

"Yeah, getting this place up and running couldn't have come at a better time," Maxwell said, crossing his arms. "We just found out my wife is pregnant."

"That's great, man." Grant clapped his friend on the shoulder. "That's an exciting time, right?"

"Yeah, it is. Well, hey. I'd love to stick around, but speaking of babies, I have to take my wife to our doctor's appointment. She's been sick, you know, so I'm gonna drive her." Maxwell backed up before turning to head for his pickup, parked not too far from the kennels on his land. "See you later, Young."

"See you."

Taking your wife to a doctor's appointment. Driving her because she's too sick to go alone. Eating frozen pizza in the living room around bottle feeds.

It was the little details that made family so amazing.

After surveying the land one more time, he headed home to his parents' house, where he'd been staying. The walls there were already closing in on him. A constant reminder of what brokenness could look like in a family.

And he could either continue that legacy of brokenness or start a new one of healing and togetherness within his own family. But how, he didn't know. Togetherness sure didn't seem possible anymore.

As he reached his parents' door, his foot brushed something on the welcome mat. A box wrapped with a bow. It was flat and long, and so he'd almost stepped on it. Grant frowned and picked it up. Turned it over in his hands. Then he noticed a strip of wrapping paper folded and taped to the present, working as a personal note.

Grant lifted the paper to read.

*For your collection of firsts. —Kallie*
*PS—Better rip the wrapping paper. Apparently the kids won't learn it from me.*

"What..." He looked around in case she was hiding in the bushes or something. Had she just dropped it off, knowing he wouldn't be there?

He stepped inside and took the present to the living room. As he sat on the couch, he ripped off the paper and took off the lid.

Inside was a whole collection of items, with a note attached to each. A photocopy of Ainsley's and Peter's footprints in the hospital. A photograph of them in their first pajamas. A couple of those little stretchy beanie hats newborns get in the hospital. A thumb drive labeled "videos of first bath, first solid food, first steps." And the plastic zipper storage bag at the bottom? Held two smaller zipper bags—each with a lock from the kids' first haircuts.

Slowly, he pulled out each item. With all the pieces laid out on the coffee table, Grant looked them over. Really studied each one, his hand over his mouth and his elbows propped on his knees. Besides the kids themselves, this was by far the coolest gift he'd ever been given. And he couldn't help but feel his throat thicken a little at the gesture.

He and Kallie had their rough patches. Neither of them was even close to perfect, and it showed too often.

But when they tried to be on the same page, they were a knockout team. Being with her and the kids could bring forth a legacy of healing, no doubt about it. And suddenly, there was nothing more that he wanted in his life than to be with her.

Except, first he'd have to convince her.

He had just the plan.

*But when I ended my marriage to your mother, I made the biggest mistake of my life. I should have fought for us, not turned into a coward and let her slip away. I loved your mother, but I was hurt. That was no excuse. You suffered the most from my mistake, and for that, I'm truly sorry.*

*When you were young, we nearly lost the farm. Too many poor seasons in a row, and I'd spent*

*too much of our savings getting the dog business
up and running. I told your mom she needed to
go find a job.*

*Back then, you couldn't work remotely like you
can now. She had to travel. At first, this worked
fine, but it wasn't long before our marriage was
strained, and I never took the necessary steps to
bring our relationship back.*

*Your family is one of the biggest legacies you
can leave your kids.*

*It doesn't matter what luxuries you have or
where you live. If the kids are safe, and your marriage is strong, and your faith in Jesus is even
stronger than all of it—then that's the legacy
worth preserving. You'll do okay.*

*I love you with all my heart. I hope you learn
what is worth preserving in this life.*
*Love,*
*Dad*

Kallie wiped her eyes and stared at his words a few
more times before finally folding the letter and clasp-
ing it close. She'd give anything for it to be her dad in
the flesh, but seeing his words and being able to read
them over and over was truly a gift.

Mom came down the narrow stairs to the living room
where Kallie sat on the sofa. In her arms was a large
tote of clothes she was taking to the laundry room. She
hadn't yet taken over the hired hand's cottage, as Grant
had suggested. Partly because she was still deciding
what she was going to do with her new freedom. Stay

here on the farm? Move into town and volunteer at the library, something she'd always wanted to do?

In the meantime, she was staying here and helping out, which Kallie couldn't have appreciated more. Until Grant had shown up, she hadn't quite realized how exhausted she'd become without help, trying to do everything on her own. Now she was seeing the benefits of asking for help and allowing that help to happen.

If only she'd realized it over a month ago, when she could have fixed things. When Grant had accused her of not letting him in, he'd been dead-on. So accurate, the truth had pinned her between the eyes, and she hadn't wanted to hear it. But the truth was, yes, she wanted Grant in her life, in their kids' lives. Problem was, she'd pushed him away, and no doubt he couldn't be convinced to come back.

Mom noticed the letter in Kallie's hands and smiled. "Reading your note from Dad?"

"Yeah. I really miss him."

Sadness crossed Mom's eyes and she set the laundry basket on the recliner before sitting down next to Kallie. "Me too, hun. I know it may not seem like it, but I really did love your father. I was just too selfish to realize it until it was too late."

That familiar burn started in Kallie's eyes, and she blinked. "I know."

"I'm sorry we made such a mess of our family." Mom shook her head, seeming to reflect on the past. "All because we wanted to chase dreams and avoid the hard stuff of life. Don't get me wrong, dreams are so important. Never forget that. I'm learning more and more that God created us with creative spirits that long to participate in amazing things. But when we pursue them at the expense of what's most important, our families and even sometimes our faith? Where's the reward in that?"

A wave of tears threatened to fall. "That's exactly what Dad was telling me in his letter."

"Now, see, your dad always was a smart man."

Kallie laughed softly. "It was right when I needed to hear it, too. I don't know how the two of your planned this little intervention, but I've gotta say, I'm impressed."

Mom laughed. "I'd say the intervention is more divine than anything else."

The smile faded from Kallie's mouth as questions took over her thoughts. "Mom? Why didn't you tell me we almost lost the farm?"

"Did your Dad tell you about that in his letter?"

"Yes. That's why you went on the road, wasn't it? To keep us here."

Mom sighed. "It started out that way. This land has been in our family for generations. It was a part of your dad, a part of me. Just like it's a part of you." She looked away. "But after a while, when things got difficult in our relationship, I found it easier to stay away. I was wrong. It wasn't fair to you or to your father."

Kallie's heart ached so much, she thought it might crumble. "I can't believe I have to sell some of it. And there's already someone interested, the Realtor says."

"What does Grant say about that?"

A huff escaped her, more hurt than anything. "Nothing, I guess. I just got a call this morning from our attorney that he removed himself from receiving any of the inheritance."

Mom frowned. "He can do that?"

"Apparently. For up to sixty days after the death or something."

"But why? What benefit is there?"

"I don't know. Probably just wants to cut ties with us, I guess."

Mom was quiet a moment. "Kallie, does that sound like him? To cut ties?"

Her heart squeezed. "This past June, I wouldn't have thought so, but—I guess that's just his default behavior. He wants to be loyal and dependable, but in the end, maybe he doesn't follow through. He left me, left the farm, left the kids."

"He comes to visit them every day. Still sits by us at church."

"Yeah, I suppose." Made no sense, though. If he wanted to be in their lives, why would he reject the inheritance? It felt like another betrayal. Which was ironic, considering her initial aversion to Grant inheriting anything in the first place. "But everyone lets you down at some point, Mom. I'm not trying to be negative—just truthful. Everyone lets you down, and this is how Grant has done it."

"You're right. Eventually, everyone will let you down. No one has a perfect record," Mom said. "But that's why we have a Savior." She traced the piping on the sofa cushion beside her. "I think regardless of everyone's imperfections, we're still called to rely on each other. I think it teaches us to let things go and offer grace when things don't work out as we'd planned."

"Letting go. I have a lot to work on in that area."

"Don't we all." Mom grinned. "Also, I think when

we fail to let go and trust in people, we ultimately are failing to let go and trust in God, and failing to reflect His goodness toward others. Allowing yourself to love means opening yourself up to pain and loss—because it will happen—but God does the same thing for us every day. In the end, love is worth the cost."

"Hmm." Interesting. And convicting. Kallie had never thought of it that way before. Was her distrust of others—like Grant—a reflection of her distrust in her Heavenly Father?

That brought her around to the question of legacy again. A word Dad had used in his letter. What legacy would she be leaving for the kids? A legacy of bitterness and stubborn independence? Or one of community and faith? The questions pressed deeply on her heart. She knew what she *wanted* her answer to be—but which one was she actually living?

In the end, it was about more than just a stretch of land.

A knock on the door interrupted her thoughts. Kallie made eye contact with her mom before they both rose to answer the door. Ruby was out on the porch, so thankfully she hadn't barked at the visitor. The kids were sleeping and weren't due to wake for a while.

Kallie opened the door and looked around. No one stood there, and Ruby was prancing through the yard, staring up the road with her tail wagging wildly. Distantly, Kallie could hear the fading rumble of a pickup engine.

She looked down and found a box at her feet. Her heart pricked with warmth.

"Someone left a package?" Mom asked, glancing around.

"Yep."

It was just a small, unadorned cardboard box, too small to even hold a pair of adult-size shoes. Like her gift, a folded strip of paper had been taped to the top.

*Since you'd only fret about ruining the wrapping paper, I didn't include any.*

Kallie bit back a giggle and opened the box. Inside, she found a large coin purse, made of soft pink leather.

"Is there anything in it?" Mom asked.

"Let's find out." Kallie wiggled her eyebrows, then opened up the purse, pulling gently on the zipper, to find a few small slips of paper inside.

She instantly recognized the shape of the first two strips she pulled out, and her heart jumped. Airplane tickets.

Mom leaned in, squinting over Kallie's shoulder as she tried to read one of them. "New York City? What's there that you want to see?"

Fighting those tears again, Kallie stared at the airline tickets. *Ellis Island.* He'd remembered.

The last strip of paper was a note. She unfolded it, easily recognizing the distinct block lettering.

*Kallie,*
*Take advantage of this time with your mom. I'll watch the kids. Go find your heritage.*
*—G*
*PS—Use this purse at the farmers market for all the money you'll rake in. I know you'll make a killing. Go get 'em.*

"So, what's with New York City?"

"It's a long story." Kallie tucked the tickets away in the purse for safekeeping. "Suffice it to say, you get to be my guest on the trip."

Mom lifted an amused brow. "Oh, I do? You don't want to go with the giver of the gift?"

An idea began to form in Kallie's mind—a crazy, harebrained idea that might have no merit, but she definitely had to check. "Mom, could you watch the kids for me while I run to town?"

for when she hits New York City? Should she tell the long-winded K9 rancher that she'd bow out of the purse fund-raising luncheon? Refuse to say yes to being a guest on the trip.

The good news was she didn't want to go. New York scared her. The city lights, the busyness, the noise made her...

## Chapter Eleven

~~

The dogs were shaping up to be fine setters indeed. Mighty fine.

After stopping by Maxwell Thornton's land to feed the dogs and get them settled in for the night, Grant drove down the street leading to his parents' house, heart light at the promise he'd seen during their training session earlier today. He'd missed getting into the grit of training. Sure, he really liked teaching other handlers what he knew. But he'd forgotten what it was like to literally be in the field, watching those dogs do their thing. It was like any other aspect of nature—witnessing the fine and elegant orchestra of instinct reminded him of the hugeness and goodness of God.

As he approached his driveway, he spotted someone sitting on the porch steps. Someone he instantly recognized. Tender face, long blond hair draped over one shoulder in a long, loose braid.

He got out of his truck and paused. "Kallie?"

She stood. "Hey."

"Are the kids okay?"

"The kids are fine. They're with Mom. I wanted to thank you for the tickets."

"No problem. Thank you for the kids' things. They're really special."

"I thought you needed something of theirs."

He stood stone still. Judging by the way she rocked back on her heels while watching him, Kallie had more to say. So he held his breath and waited.

"What happened to the job in North Dakota?"

"Didn't take it."

"But why?"

"I told you. I'm not leaving the kids." *Or you.*

Kallie swallowed, took a step forward. "I was going to tell you we'd like to follow you there."

Grant's brows peaked. "What? Really?"

"I've been acting foolish. I realized it the first time I saw your empty cottage and the pickup missing out front. No one stopping in for morning coffee. The kids' dad not helping me bathe them and put them to bed. Neither Mom nor I can read *Goodnight Moon* quite like you can."

A corner of Grant's mouth ticked into a smile.

"And it's not just because you gave me plane tickets or the money bag, which were both super thoughtful. Or even the fact that I just found out from the real estate agent that you're the one trying to buy my land—"

"Wow, so much for privacy."

"Grant." She tried to hide that beautiful smile, but it found its way onto her face anyway. "Your name is right there on the purchase agreement. And anyway, I'm trying to apologize here."

"Sorry. Proceed."

She laughed. Then her features sobered. "How did you pay for the plane tickets?"

He pursed his lips before answering. "Dog training money."

"And the land?"

Grant didn't answer.

"You sold your car, didn't you? Then rejected your inheritance so you could buy it instead, which was the only way I could have enough money to pay off Dad's debt, yet still keep the land." Tears trailed down her lovely face. She took another step toward him. "How could you do that?"

He shrugged. "It needed to stay in the family."

"Our legacy to our kids and future generations is rooted deeper than land. I think that's what Dad wanted us to understand. I think he wanted us to be a family. I see that now." She stepped right up to him, merely a foot away. "I was so very wrong. About everything. I didn't deserve your kindness and yet you gave it to me anyway. You belong in our lives, Grant. I'm terrible at getting my feelings out, but I'm going to work on that." She reached out for both of his hands. "So hear me when I say this—I love you."

Wow. Air released from his lungs. Letting go of her hands, he slid his arms around her. "You do, huh?"

"Mmm-hmm."

"Well, I guess the feeling's mutual then."

"Oh?"

"Yes, ma'am. I love you, Kallie Shore. I have from the very beginning, and I'm sorry I got lost along the way."

"I get it."

"But don't mistake what I'm about to tell you," he said, hoping the look he gave her communicated the truth he felt deep in his bones. "I need you. Not just for the farm. Not just for the kids. For myself. And I promise to spend the rest of my life proving it to you."

Questions seemed to languish in her eyes as hope replaced them. "And I need you, too. No more trying to run our family on my own."

Music to his ears. "Be careful what you promise, there, Kal. Don't go losing your stubborn streak." He winked and tugged her closer. "Your determination and bossiness are some of the things I love most about you."

Breaking into a grin, Kallie hugged his neck. "Then you listen here, Grant Young. I'm expecting you for breakfast tomorrow morning at eight o'clock sharp. It's eggs and pancakes, and don't you be late."

His brows ticked in amusement. He sure loved that gal.

"Yes, ma'am," he said before giving her a kiss.

"Does that mean you'll move back to the farm?" she murmured against his lips.

He chuckled. "Only on one condition."

"Which is?"

"You have to bake a whole lot more pies. And not just for the farmers market."

Her blue eyes glittered. "I think that can be arranged."

"Oh, actually, there's a second condition, too."

"Okay, what?"

"You have to open another present."

She grinned. "Okay, show me where it is."

"It's not wrapped, but I'm guessing you'll be fine

with that." He reached into the pocket of his jeans and fished out a small silk bag with its drawstring pulled tight.

He handed it over, and Kallie's eyes widened.

She loosened the drawstring and let his grandmother's ring slide into the palm of her hand.

Kallie raised her gaze, rich and searching. "How long have you been carrying this around?"

"Off and on since Nebraska. I picked it up from Mom while we were there." Lacing her fingers with his, he closed her hand around the ring. "So will you, Kallie Shore? Marry me and be my wife?"

Those long lashes blinked overtop blushing cheeks before she looked up at him, gaze glittering. "Only on one condition of my own. I'm going to need a lot of help with the kids if I'm going to be spending time in the kitchen making pies for my new husband."

He gently cupped her jawline in his hands, caressing her cheeks with his thumbs. He never knew one person could make him both so mad and so awestruck in the same lifetime. In the same week. But that was real romance, wasn't it? "Oh, I'm planning on it, darlin'. And I wouldn't miss it for the world."

# Epilogue

Ruby sounded the alarm that Grant's truck was pulling into the turnaround—as did Lola and all her four pups, Lew, Hunter, Dash and Point. The six of them gathered at the screen door for their nightly routine of welcoming Grant home.

September heat came through the screen door, but rain would be upon them soon, and Kallie loved the smell of an impending storm. As long as there wasn't any hail.

"Okay, okay." She wove through the wiggly pups and opened the screen door, allowing them to propel themselves off the porch and down the walkway. She grinned, watching their enthusiasm for a minute before returning inside.

Adding five dogs to the family was quite the adventure—it made nine dogs in total. But when Grant had adopted them from Helping Hands in order to give them a good home, and then gave them to Kallie as a wedding gift, she couldn't imagine saying no. Now they were just as vital to the Bitter Creek Farm operations as everyone else.

As for all the other dogs at Helping Hands, Grant had called his large list of clients, as well as all the operations who'd hired him to give seminars this past year. Amazingly enough, he'd secured an adoption for each and every dog the facility had.

"Now," Kallie said, whirling back into the house. "Places, everyone!"

Peter and Ainsley, now sixteen months old, gave her huge, semi-tooth-filled grins as they stood in the living room. As she strode toward them, they let out a burst of high-anticipation giggles and tried their very best to climb up onto the sofa. Not that they were successful— yet. But it was coming, quicker than quick.

"Okay, Daddy's coming," Kallie announced, wrangling each kid and helping them get up on the sofa. "Remember what I said. When Daddy comes in, we have to sit still."

They laughed and squirmed, completely amused by this new game.

Kallie heard the door open and quickly sat the kids upright. "Hey!" she said, scurrying into the kitchen. She planted a kiss on Grant's lips before tugging him into the living room. "I have a surprise for you."

"Another pie?"

She shook her head. She'd already made enough of those to fill a lifetime. "Okay, kids. What did we learn to say today? Say Daddy."

But when she turned to the kids, Peter simply waved…and Ainsley had disappeared.

The wording on his white T-shirt made no sense without his sister.

Grant chased her down before she could climb the stairs. Pleased to be picked up, she nestled into Grant's shoulder like she was finally home. And she really was. Because Grant was her daddy. That man's arms provided shelter and grace like no one else's.

He did that for her, too.

With a bout of tickling, Grant plopped Ainsley back on the sofa. "Say Daddy!" he said, bringing forth more giggles. Then he stopped and listened.

"Daddy!" Ainsley cried out, arms flying into the air. Laughing, she squirmed away and tried to get down again.

"Park it, sweetie pie!" Kallie plopped on the sofa between the two kiddos and scooped one onto each leg. She wouldn't be able to do that for much longer. "Peter, say Daddy."

Peter gave a shy smile, chewing on a finger. "Daddy," he murmured, quiet but proud.

She didn't think Grant could shine any brighter. "Nice work, kiddos," he said. "It's all I ever wanted."

Kallie rolled her eyes. She repositioned the wiggly kids on her lap. "Now, Daddy, do you like our new shirts?"

She couldn't read them with the kids on her lap, but she already knew them by heart. Peter's shirt said "Gonna be," and Ainsley's shirt said "big siblings."

Grant read them, and his eyes widened. "Seriously?"

"Yep." Kallie couldn't help but grin as she stood and let the kids scramble off the sofa to freedom. "I'm sure."

Beaming, Grant swung her around in his arms.

"That's the best news I've heard in a long time," he said. "When?"

"May sometime."

"Just like these two."

Kallie smiled. "Yeah, I suppose so. Guess it'll be a busy month."

"Maybe we'll have two again." Grant laughed at Kallie's wary stare. "Hey, you never know."

"What I *do* know, Grant Young," Kallie said, sidling up to him and slipping her arms around his torso, "is that I'm the most blessed wife in all of South Dakota. You are the father I've always wanted for my children. And the husband I always wanted, too."

"Back at ya," he said with a wink, sliding his thumb tenderly along her cheek. "I couldn't ask for a more amazing wife."

For thirteen months, these kids' family circle had consisted of Kallie's Dad and her. She had convinced herself that it was all Peter and Ainsley needed. But seeing them with Grant and everyone else who'd recently come into their lives had opened Kallie's heart to new possibilities. To new promises.

To the incredibly rich tapestry of family.

Life was good.

* * * * *

*If you enjoyed this book,*
*be sure to check out these other titles*

Finding the Road Home *by Tina Radcliffe*
The Texan's Promise *by Jolene Navarro*
The Cowboy's Unexpected Baby *by Stephanie Dees*

*Available now from Love Inspired!*

*Find more great reads at* www.LoveInspired.com

Dear Reader,

What words can I use to express my gratitude? You are the reason I write, and it is my prayer to always deliver a story to you that is heartfelt and God-honoring. I hope I've served the Lord with Grant and Kallie's story and that you find hope in the midst of these pages.

Life is messy and difficult, and we need each other to get through it. And being successful in life isn't about gaining control. It's about surrendering to the Father. His grace is sufficient for us, after all. And His strength is made perfect in our weakness. This is what Grant and Kallie learn as they fall in love a second time.

It's a truth I hope you embrace as well. You are loved by an Almighty Savior, and if you follow Him, His grace is sufficient for you, too.

I'd love to connect with you, dear reader. You can find me on Facebook @AuthorJanetteForeman, on Twitter @AuthorJanetteF, on Instagram @AuthorJanetteForeman, and on Pinterest. And if you'd love more book news, freebies, and other fun things, you can sign up for my newsletter at www.JanetteForeman.com/author-news.

Sincerely,
*Janette Foreman*

## SPECIAL EXCERPT FROM

## ❧ LOVE INSPIRED
### INSPIRATIONAL ROMANCE

*Temporarily in her Amish community to help with her
sick brother's business, nurse Rachel Blank can't wait
to get back to the* Englisch *world...and far away from
Arden Esh. Her brother's headstrong carpentry partner
challenges her at every turn. But when a family crisis
redefines their relationship, will Rachel realize the life
she really wants is right here...with Arden?*

*Read on for a sneak preview of*
The Amish Nurse's Suitor *by Carrie Lighte,
available April 2020 from Love Inspired.*

The soup scalded Arden's tongue and gave him something to
distract himself from the topsy-turvy way he was feeling. As he
chugged down half a glass of milk, Rachel remarked how tired
Ivan still seemed.

"*Jah*, he practically dozed off midsentence in his room."

"I'll have to wake him soon for his medication. And to check
for a fever. They said to watch for that. A relapse of pneumonia
can be even worse than the initial bout."

"You're going to need endurance, too."

"What?"

"You prayed I'd have endurance. You're going to need it, too,"
Arden explained. "There were a lot of nurses in the hospital, but
here you're on your own."

"Don't you think I'm qualified to take care of him by myself?"

That wasn't what he'd meant at all. Arden was surprised
by the plea for reassurance in Rachel's question. Usually, she
seemed so confident. "I can't think of anyone better qualified to

LIEXP0320

take care of him. But he's got a long road to recovery ahead, and you're going to need help so you don't wear yourself out."

"I told Hadassah I'd *wilkom* her help, but I don't think I can count on her. Joyce and Albert won't return from Canada for a couple more weeks, according to Ivan."

"In addition to Grace, there are others in the community who will be *hallich* to help."

"I don't know about that. I'm worried they'll stay away because of my presence. Maybe Ivan would have been better off without me here. Maybe my coming here was a mistake."

"*Neh*. It wasn't a mistake." Upon seeing the fragile vulnerability in Rachel's eyes, Arden's heart ballooned with compassion. "Trust me, the community will *kumme* to help."

"In that case, I'd better keep dessert and tea on hand," Rachel said, smiling once again.

"Does that mean we can't have a slice of that pie over there?"

"Of course it doesn't. And since Ivan has no appetite, you and I might as well have large pieces."

Supping with Rachel after a hard day's work, encouraging her and discussing Ivan's care as if he were…not a child, but *like* a child, felt… Well, it felt like how Arden always imagined it would feel if he had a family of his own. Which was probably why, half an hour later as he directed his horse toward home, Arden's stomach was full, but he couldn't shake the aching emptiness he felt inside.

*She is going back, so I'd better not get too accustomed to her company, as pleasant as it's turning out to be.*

*Don't miss*
The Amish Nurse's Suitor *by Carrie Lighte,*
*available April 2020 wherever*
Love Inspired *books and ebooks are sold.*

LoveInspired.com